SWEET HARVEST

Lisa Ann Verge

A KISMET™ Romance

METEOR PUBLISHING CORPORATION
Bensalem, Pennsylvania

To Rita B., Maria F., Sarah G.,
Layle G., and Rita R.
for all those Tuesday nights
of honesty and laughter.

LISA ANN VERGE

Twenty-nine-year-old Lisa Ann Verge is already the author of three award-winning historical romance novels. A "Vassar Girl" who once worked as an environmental chemist, Lisa is an intrepid traveler who has explored Europe and Canada, sometimes solo and often with no more luggage than a backpack. She has lived in Boston, Manhattan, and San Francisco, but, currently, she makes her home just north of New York City with her husband, Tom, and her newborn daughter, Caitlin.

ONE

He was certifiably insane.

Amanda Karlson was a chemist, not a psychiatrist, but this diagnosis required no medical degree. There was simply no other way to describe a man, clad in nothing but black spandex, clinging like a human fly to the sizzling face of a granite cliff.

Amanda adjusted her sunglasses against the blinding August sun. She pulled a stray tress of white-blond hair out of her face as a dusty breeze swirled around her. He *was* crazy. The cliff, sheer and gleaming, towered over the scattered redwood buildings of the Cedar Ridge Winery. No ropes dangled over the edge. No hooks or spikes jutted from the granite. Nothing kept the climber on the cliff face but brute strength.

And sheer audacity.

The hot earth burned through the soles of her flat leather shoes as she stood in the open sun. She had come all the way up to these hills surrounding Napa Valley just for a business meeting—yet the only living soul she found on the grounds of the winery was a half-naked, bare-handed mountain climber. Amanda raked her fingers through her straight, shoulder-length hair, trying to make sense of the day's latest development. The whole morning had been a series of surprises, one right after another. She didn't like surprises—or anything random and unpredictable and unexpected. Surprises upset the natural order of things . . . and they were usually bad news.

It had all started with a single morning phone call. She knew better than to take any calls before her third cup of coffee—but this was the one call she couldn't resist, for the man on the other end claimed he represented the Cedar Ridge Winery, the same winery that had been sold recently to an undisclosed buyer—the same winery she had been trying, in vain, to buy grapes from for years. Of *course* she climbed in her old pickup and made the trip to this narrow ravine in the hills. No wine chemist in all of Napa would refuse the opportunity to discuss a "business proposition" with someone from Cedar Ridge. She just didn't expect to find the place as quiet as a monastery, at a time when every winery in California was preparing for "crush," the annual harvesting and pressing of grapes. To top it all off, there was no sign of the mysterious representative, Garrick Kane. The only man who *was* here was a bronzed demigod, with an exaggerated faith in the strength of his knuckle bones, shimmying down the sheer face of a cliff.

Amanda grasped the lapel of her emerald-green suit jacket and flapped it, trying to create a cool draft against her damp skin. She was as crazy as this lunatic to stand here in the open sun; for whatever reason, Mr. Kane obviously wasn't coming. From what she had seen through the dirty windows of the winery, it looked like no one had stepped foot in the place since Mr. Brunichelli, the previous owner, had died last spring. Besides, if she lingered much longer, the cursedly sensitive skin of her nose would blister like a fried egg on hot pavement.

As she turned to return to her pickup, the climber's foot slipped. She sucked in a swift breath as pebbles skittered down the face of the cliff to scatter across the ground. His thigh, rock hard from the exertion, quivered under the force of his weight. He searched for a sliver of granite with the toe of his free foot, then, finding it, he wedged his sneaker in, bobbed carefully, and slid down a small distance. He dipped one of his hands into a cup of chalk slung around his waist, then calmly wedged his whitened fingers back into a shadowed crease.

Lord have mercy.

She couldn't leave. This winery was utterly abandoned except for her and this crazed climber. And as finely honed as he was, all the muscles in the world couldn't cushion a fall to this hard, pebble-strewn driveway. If she left him here and he slipped, it could be weeks before anyone found him. Besides, she reasoned, when he made it to the ground—God willing—he might be able to tell her something about the missing Mr. Kane. At least then this trip up the mountains wouldn't be a complete waste of time.

She watched him as he made his way down the face of the cliff, as sleek and sure as a cat, the muscles of his thighs and arms rigid and gleaming. A faint flush suffused her cheeks as her thoughts strayed. My Lord, had it been so long since she'd seen a good-looking man that she was reduced to ogling a complete stranger? She thought back through the accountants and electricians and used-car salesmen her best friend at Windsor, Maggie Johnson, constantly paraded before her as potential dates. Well, perhaps it had been some time since she'd seen anyone who didn't sport a well-inflated spare tire. She never really noticed before because she never really cared. Amanda couldn't seem to make Maggie understand that she really wasn't looking for a soul mate, even if she was single and—God forbid!—*thirty* years of age. Amanda had her career—something stable and secure and completely dependable. Something that wouldn't wrench her heart out by the roots.

"Well, hello."

She started abruptly and looked up. The climber had already finished his descent and stood at the base of the cliff, staring at her. She wondered if it were possible for the temperature to increase ten degrees in ten seconds.

He had Warren Beatty eyes—bright, sleepy-lidded, and sensual. A bristle of stubble spotted his square jaw. His dark hair clung to his forehead and the back of his neck. As he looked at her, his lips spread in a grin, the kind of pure-white lopsided smile that belonged on a baseball player or on the cover of a dentist's magazine.

"If I had known I had such a lovely audience," he said, as he walked toward a silver Saab parked beside the wine cellar, "I might have climbed higher."

"Thank God you didn't know."

She blurted the words out, then promptly frowned at herself. She never blurted. Her associates in work called her the Ice Queen behind her back because she was so cool under pressure.

"It's not as treacherous as it looks. This rock is just training ground for when I go back to Yosemite."

"I see." Her eyes widened behind the shade of her sunglasses. She remembered the sheer granite cliffs of Yosemite canyon from a camping trip she had taken with some friends a few years ago. "I take it you do this professionally?"

"God, no." He pulled a bottle of spring water out of a bag which lay open on the trunk of his car. "I do this for fun. It clears my head."

She wondered what else this man did for "fun," and suspected it included sky diving, or surfing in the shark-infested waters off the coast of San Francisco. She also wondered what problems he needed to clear from his head at noon on a normal working day.

"It's not so bad," he said, reading her expression, amusement glinting in his eyes. "You risk more climbing into your car every morning."

"Personally, the closest I like to get to death is between the pages of a mystery novel." She glanced askance at the height of the cliff, then looked pointedly at him. "At least when I read alone, all I risk is a paper cut."

"I wasn't alone." He wiped his forehead with his muscled forearm. "You were here."

She didn't bother to point out that he had no way of knowing she was going to be here. Any man who scaled peaks with his bare hands wouldn't listen to that kind of logic. He lifted the water to his lips and let the excess pour around his mouth and splash over his shoulders. She could almost hear his skin sizzling from the contact. Or perhaps it was all those overheated muscles, bulging obscenely beneath the skimpy bodysuit from the exertion of the climb.

"You should get out of the sun before you fry that

fair Nordic skin." He screwed the cap on the bottle of water. "Come join me in the shade."

Amanda hesitated. She hadn't been so isolated from the dating scene that she didn't recognize an invitation when she heard it . . . and saw it in his eyes. This man was offering her more than protection from the sun. He was offering her a chance to get to know him better.

Her internal temperature edged a few degrees higher. She plucked at the lapel of her suit jacket. She was definitely wading in unfamiliar waters. This climber wasn't the sweet, brotherly type of man Maggie usually fixed her up with. His raw sexual magnetism was as palpable as the waves of heat rising from the earth beneath her feet. She felt a little like a sliver of metal coming too close to an extremely powerful magnet. One more step . . . and she'd be sucked in.

So she backed away.

"I really have to go." She pointed vaguely behind her, toward her pickup truck parked in the driveway next to the main building. "I just wanted to stay until you were safely on the ground—"

"You can't leave yet. We haven't even talked."

He put down the bottle of water and crossed the distance that separated them. He held out his hand. Automatically, she gave him hers. His palm was damp, gritty, calloused, and rough, like the surface of a cat's tongue. The touch was strangely erotic, as was the unabashedly male scent of his sun-warmed skin.

"You're one hell of a surprise." His gaze roamed from the top of her blond head to the length of her long, pale legs. "Frankly, I didn't think they made wine chemists who looked like you, Amanda Karlson."

The sound of her name jarred against her ears. "Excuse me?"

"I thought they all wore horn-rimmed glasses and white coats. Thank God for women's lib." He shook her hand firmly. "Garrick Kane, at your service."

Amanda's stomach dropped to her toes. She snatched her hand out of his and quickly adjusted her sunglasses. This tall, muscular, sweaty, blindingly handsome creature was Garrick Kane? *Garrick Kane of the Cedar Ridge Winery?* She stared at him, at the sweat and spring water dripping over his naked shoulders into the U of his bodysuit. It couldn't be . . . She felt a cold frisson of dread. She couldn't have spent the last fifteen minutes openly ogling a potential client.

She pulled up her sleeve and glanced at her watch, not really seeing the dial. "I was under the impression we had a meeting at noon, Mr. Kane."

"Garrick." The smile returned, slow, easy, and utterly unapologetic. "Yes, we do have an appointment."

"I've been waiting for you for a half hour." She forcefully pulled her gaze above the level of his neck. "In fact, I searched the whole winery for you."

"You found me."

"I was looking for a man who was meeting me for a business appointment." She smoothed the palm of her hand over her hip, trying to dry it free of perspiration, of the feel of his touch. "Frankly, I thought *you* were a trespassing lunatic."

"I tend to lose track of time when I climb. A bad habit, but not my worst." He touched her elbow and turned toward the main house. "Come on. Let's go inside, out of this heat. Maybe I can appease you with a cold beer."

"Just one minute. . . ." Amanda dug her heels into the ground and felt a spurt of defiance. This was one surprise too many. How many people did she know in the wine business who climbed rocks bare-handed for fun? How many people showed up for meetings dressed like Arnold Schwarzenegger in training? And this man—she took a breath to slow her pulse rate—this man certainly didn't look like he belonged working in a winery, in *any* capacity. He looked like he could hew stone with his bare hands.

She skillfully worked her arm free. "Mr. Kane, you understand that any business dealings have to start with an element of trust, correct?"

He looked at her quizzically. "Well, yes, I suppose—"

"I came all the way up here in the middle of the day during the busiest part of the season, on the promise of an undefined 'business proposition,' only to find you playing Spiderman."

"Spiderman?"

"Face it, Mr. Kane, in that outfit you don't exactly exude great business sense."

He looked down at the body-fitting suit, and then up at her sleek green outfit. One corner of his lips tilted. "This *is* California, isn't it? I was under the impression that three-piece suits were banned west of the Rockies."

"They're not. And frankly, if it were anywhere near my birthday and if you were wearing another layer of clothing, I'd suspect you were a male stripper hired by some prankster for my entertainment. But since you're already stripped to the bare essentials," Amanda continued, forging ahead, ignoring his sound of surprise, "I assume that theory is incorrect, and there might still be a kernel of authenticity in this whole setup."

"A male stripper, huh?" He placed his hands on his hips, a grin stretching from ear to ear. "Do you think I could make a living out of it?"

"Frankly, Mr. Kane, first I'd have to see you dance."

The minute the words left her lips, Amanda wished she hadn't said them. Her tongue was running a mile ahead of her brain. She still half expected him to pull a tape deck out of his gym bag and start stripping bare of all that spandex in the open air—that certainly would be a lot more believable than having this sweaty, virile creature be associated with the winery somehow. "So, you see, before I walk into an abandoned building with you," she continued brazenly, "I want to know who you are, and what your relationship is with Cedar Ridge."

Something sparkled in his eyes. "Miguel didn't tell me you had a sense of humor."

Amanda lifted a brow. Miguel was the name of the vineyardist of Cedar Ridge under Mr. Brunichelli. "Miguel Juarez?"

"He told me you were one of the few winemakers in the region who 'respected his harvest,' whatever that means."

That sounded like Miguel, she thought, and she vaguely remembered that Garrick Kane *had* mentioned his name on the phone this morning. She could just imagine what else Miguel had to say. A year or two younger than Amanda, the vineyardist was known as an incorrigible Don Juan. For years he had been trying to talk her into a date, and she had flatly refused each time. "How well do you know Miguel?"

"I hired him." His grin spread wickedly. "I'm the new owner of Cedar Ridge."

What precious equilibrium she had regained since encountering Garrick suddenly spun off into infinity. His statement was so preposterous that she knew it was true. Only the owner of the winery would have the raw nerve to summon a stranger to a business meeting and then arrive dressed like a wrestler. Amanda fervently wished the earth would open up and swallow her—not an idle prayer for a woman who had spent most of her adult life near the San Andreas Fault.

"You're the third person in Napa to know," he continued. "The other two are in my employ."

"You've been the main source of gossip in Napa for weeks. There are journalists all over the valley who would pay a hefty sum to know your name—"

"And I'm trusting you to keep this information under wraps for a little longer." He tilted his head, urging her to face him. "You see, I've trusted you with my deepest secret, Amanda Karlson. Will you come into the house now?" His lips twitched. "If I promise to keep my clothes on?"

"Of course I'll come in." She tugged firmly on the hem of her suit jacket and flashed him a glare. "You should have told me you were the owner on the phone this morning."

"For the sake of my privacy, the fewer people who know, the better. Besides, if I told you, it would have defeated my purpose. I wanted to see how adventuresome you were." His eyes twinkled. "You didn't disappoint me."

His laughter drifted back to her as he turned and headed toward the rear entrance of the house. She readjusted her sunglasses, which kept slipping down her nose. The situation had taken a 180-degree turn. No longer was she dealing with a virile, attractive rock-climbing trespasser, but now she was going to negotiate with the new owner of Cedar Ridge. She tore her gaze away from his flexing muscles as he climbed the back stairs of the winery and entered the redwood building. She had to shut off these hormones. She could no longer consider Garrick Kane a man—only a business associate.

Cool it, Amanda. You've dealt with good-looking men before.

She had—a hundred times. Just because she had met Garrick Kane in unusual circumstances, just because sensuality seemed to ooze out of his pores, didn't mean she couldn't still relate to him on a professional level. She simply had to cork up her own unexpected—and purely physical—attraction to him and pretend it had never happened.

She took a deep breath and started by focusing on why she was here—or, at least, why she *thought* she was here. For years, she had been trying to convince the late owner of Cedar Ridge to sell his grapes to the Windsor Winery, ever since he stopped making wine and put his premium grapes on the open market. But old Mr. Brunichelli always sold to the highest bidder— usually some huge conglomerate that made common jug wine. No matter how many special deals she offered, how many incentives, Mr. Brunichelli wouldn't sell to anyone who couldn't match the highest bid. It would be the coup of the season if she could land a contract to buy the Cedar Ridge grapes. All she had to do was keep her wits about her, her eyes above chin level— and not let Garrick Kane pull the rug out from under her feet again.

Garrick led her down the hall of the main building. The house smelled like lemon polish and antiseptic. Boxes cluttered the floor. She maneuvered around the debris and entered a bare kitchen. Two wide windows with western exposure bathed the room and all its white pine cabinets in bright light.

He pulled two imported beers out of the refrigerator and held them up to her. "Have a preference?"

"No."

He started to close the door, still clutching the two beers.

"No—I mean, I'd rather not have a beer."

He grinned. "Well, I know it's not because you don't drink on the job. I suppose I should have offered you wine, but believe it or not, I don't have any."

"Water would be fine." *To wipe the taste of shoe leather out of my mouth.* "Lots of ice."

When he handed her the chilled glass, she took a sip and felt the icy liquid ease her parched throat. She looked up and found his eyes upon her, curious and intense. He reached out and pulled her sunglasses from her face.

She blinked a few times in the light. She took the sunglasses from him and grasped them in her fist. "I suppose I don't need these indoors, do I?"

He studied her face intently, and for the first time she saw his eyes without the distortion of her shades. They were deep blue, like the color of dark sapphires. His lashes were long, too, long and dark.

"Green," he murmured. "Somehow I thought they'd be blue, but they're not. They're pale green. Nice."

She lowered her lids sharply, trying to hide the effect his words had on her jumpy, overactive libido. This was not at all like the meeting of two professionals. She had to bring the situation back under control—and to find some solid footing.

"This meeting has already been delayed, Mr. Kane, and there are people at Windsor who are wondering where I am right now." She met his gaze evenly. "Perhaps we should get down to business?"

He shrugged, and waved for her to begin.

"This proposition you mentioned on the phone this morning," she began. "It wouldn't have anything to do with rock-climbing, would it?"

"Only in that both are challenges." He cracked open the beer and leaned against the counter. "Do you like challenges, Amanda?"

She started. Her name sounded intimate on his lips—rough and husky and endearing. "I'm afraid I limit my challenges to whatever can be accomplished on solid ground."

"That's a broad enough field." He took a sip of the beer and wiped his mouth with the back of his forearm. "How long have you been working at Windsor?"

"Four years. The last two I've been an assistant winemaker under André Bonchemin."

Amanda watched his face at the mention of the renowned winemaster's name, but nothing registered in his eyes. Nothing more than the same obvious, intense scrutiny that had been in their dark-blue depths since he first looked at her.

"Miguel tells me you know a lot about this vineyard."

"I know a lot about most of the vineyards in the region." She shrugged, trying to ease the awkward tension that grew between them. She rubbed the glass of water against her chest, letting the condensation cool the area where the sun had burned a V into her skin. "At Windsor, I'm in charge of buying the best Napa grapes for our vintage wines, so it's my business."

"Then these are good vineyards?"

She raised a brow. He *had* to know the worth of the

vines, if he really owned the place—every winemaker in Napa lusted after the venerated grapes of Cedar Ridge. She wondered if he was testing her in some way—if that was the reason for the inscrutable expression on his face. "The best chardonnay grapes in the entire valley grow up here, on the morning slopes. And because of the microclimate of the ravine, you also have some of the finest cabernet." When he waited, expectant, for her to continue, she launched into a detailed discussion of the Cedar Ridge vines. She explained that because the vines were planted on thin soil and mountain slopes, they had to struggle more to bear fruit. The result was small, thick-skinned grapes which created powerful and intense flavors in wine. The tension in her body eased as she warmed to her subject. Winemaking was her first love, born in the musty confines of a barn in Massachusetts, where she and her father used to crush the native concord grapes the old-fashioned way and make sweet, potent family wine. Then, the whole process had seemed like magic to her. Now, having studied the process for years, she knew better—but despite the years of sacrifice and hard work, winemaking had never lost its allure.

She glanced at Mr. Kane and realized she was telling him too much—she was praising his grapes to the stars. She wasn't likely to land a good contract if she didn't set her mind on business. *Think price, Amanda. If it's too high, Windsor won't go for it.* "Of course, with all these trees around," she hedged, "your yields aren't very good. You've got to share your harvest with the birds."

"I see."

"But any competent winemaker knows that," she

continued swiftly, "and sacrifices some tonnage for quality."

"Do you play much tennis, Amanda?"

"Tennis?" She stared at him, nonplussed at the sudden change in subject. "I don't have time for tennis."

His Warren Beatty eyes rolled over her. "How do you manage to keep in shape then, drinking wine all day?"

"I don't—" She shook her head in frustration. He was doing it again, focusing all that masculinity on her like a spotlight. "There's a difference between drinking and tasting wine, Mr. Kane. If I drank wine all day, I'd be drunk every night."

"You look like the tennis type. You should take it up. I'm looking for a partner."

"I don't have much time to play tennis, or any sport." She tightened her grip on the glass. "I take my work very seriously."

"That's obvious." He shifted his position, leaning one elbow against the counter so that his face was nearly level with hers. "What I want to know is, what do you do when you leave work?"

She put the glass down with a clatter. The conversation was swiftly slipping out of her control. He was doing nothing to hide his interest in her, no matter how professional she tried to be. He was also looking at her as if she were another mountain he'd like to climb.

She had to put a stop to this immediately. "*Mr.* Kane—"

"Garrick."

"—I don't see what my outside interests have to do with your proposition." She stepped slightly away from him. "In fact, what kind of proposition *are* you offering?"

"Originally, I had one idea." He placed his beer beside her glass. "Looking at you, I'm getting a whole lot of others."

Amanda sucked in her breath, shocked and flattered at the same time, and even more shocked at herself for feeling flattered at his obvious advances. She knew she should leave. She should turn around, find her way out of this house, get into her pickup, and go back to Windsor. She'd already spent too much time away from her responsibilities. Besides, whatever this man had in mind, it had little to do with selling grapes to the Windsor Winery. And no matter how heart-stoppingly handsome he was, the fact that he was the owner of a winery made any other type of relationship completely out of the question. Amanda Karlson never, *ever* got involved with anyone in the business.

But her feet stuck to the floor. She told herself it was because the possibility of a contract with Cedar Ridge was too ripe a plum. She couldn't leave, not yet, not without finding out exactly why he had called her here. She stiffened her spine to take full advantage of her five feet eight inches. "I'd like to hear the original idea, Mr. Kane. I'm not interested in the others."

"Don't misunderstand me, Amanda—I didn't mean to offend you." He straightened from the counter and ran his hand through his damp hair. "I have a bad habit of saying exactly what's on my mind. You're a beautiful woman. Would you prefer I act the hypocrite and pretend I didn't notice?"

Yes. Hypocrisy she could deal with—she dealt with it every day. Honest attraction was a lot more unnerving.

"As I told you earlier," he said, his voice suddenly becoming brisk, "I just bought this winery. I didn't know much about its history until I got here. Apparently it's been some time since wine has been produced here.''

"It has been three years," she answered, her mind still reeling. "Mr. Brunichelli was too sick to run the winery, and his heirs squabbled so much after he died that they just sold the place.''

"Did you know this Mr. Brunichelli?"

"No." She forced herself to meet his eyes, to ignore the current running between them. "This is a small community. Gossip flies fast. Everyone knows everyone else's business.''

"I see."

"Mr. Brunichelli sold his grapes in the last few years," she continued, trying to veer the conversation onto safe ground. "Good grapes bring good prices. With so many small wineries on the verge of bankruptcy, it's a logical alternative to winemaking.''

"So I've heard. But I didn't buy a winery to sell off the vineyard grapes. I want to revitalize the place. This year.''

Amanda raised her brows. "Harvest starts in two weeks.''

"So I've been told. The winery's already equipped to make wine. And you admitted yourself that these are some of the best vineyards in the region.''

She nodded, wondering what in God's name he was driving at.

"All I need now is an expert winemaker to make those grapes into premier wine." He leaned back and spread his hands on the counter. "I want that winemaker to be you, Amanda Karlson.''

TWO

Amanda's sunglasses slipped through her fingers, bounced off her foot, and clattered across the floor, sliding to a stop in the middle of a patch of sunlight.

She hardly noticed. She felt like one of those blow-up punching dolls, wobbling wildly on her feet. She took a deep breath, trying to regain her bearings. She must have misunderstood. Garrick Kane could not just have offered her the position of winemaster at Cedar Ridge.

"Run that by me one more time, Mr. Kane. I'm not sure I heard you correctly."

"I think you did." His lips tilted as he bent to retrieve the fallen sunglasses. "I'm glad you weren't holding your glass when I told you or we'd be knee-deep in shards."

Numbly, she took the sunglasses he offered and gripped them tightly in her hands. He smelled like sweat and clean air and sunshine, a heady, undeniably male mixture. She searched his eyes for something—

laughter, mischief—something that would tip her off that this offer wasn't real, but all she saw was gentle teasing, and a smoky sensuality. She twisted away. It was bad enough her head was spinning—she didn't need her senses swimming, too. Garrick Kane was churning up her emotions like the rotor of a blender.

She heard him straighten behind her and walk to the opposite counter. "I know this isn't the Windsor Winery," he said. "It doesn't have all the glossy machinery you're probably used to, and I've been told we can only produce twelve thousand cases of wine a year. But you won't be an assistant winemaker here. You'll be in charge of everything in the cellar. You'll be creating the wines yourself." He paused. "And whatever Windsor is paying you, I guarantee I'll offer you more. Much more."

She closed her eyes, scarcely believing his words. The money was important—it had always been—but she was too much in shock from his offer for anything else to register. Winemaster of the Cedar Ridge Winery! For so long, she had carefully mapped out her career. Her degree in enology from the University of California at Davis had gotten her foot in the door at the Windsor Winery. Her hard work and determination had made her an assistant winemaker under André Bonchemin, one of the most skilled and renowned enologists in California. The next logical step in her career was either to succeed to André's position—an unlikely event, for the robust Frenchman loved his work and had no plans for retirement despite his advanced age—or to become the winemaker of a small winery. She had been prepared to wait, for opportunities such as these were as rare and precious as 1936 Georges de Latour Private Reserve.

Garrick Kane had just tossed the opportunity in her lap as if it were nothing more than a bauble.

What would Dad say about this? she wondered, fiddling distractedly with her sunglasses. She'd come a long way for a farm girl from Massachusetts. She had always wanted to control her own wine cellar—Lord, what winemaker wouldn't?—but the opportunity had always seemed like the brass ring on a merry-go-round. Within her sight, but just out of her reach.

Suddenly, she knew what Dad would say. She heard his voice in her head as clearly as if he were standing beside her in this kitchen and had not been dead for the past sixteen years.

She turned and met Garrick's smoky gaze, summoning her scattered wits. "My father had a phrase, Mr. Kane. He used to say, 'Amanda girl, if someone tries to sell you a magic hat, before you buy it, check up his sleeve.' "

He smiled and spread his bare, brawny arms. "Feel free."

She frowned and tried in vain not to imagine what it would be like to run her hands over his warm, hard body, to feel the crispness of his dark chest hair between her fingers. "There are dozens of other qualified winemakers in the valley who would snap up this offer like starving dogs after raw meat," she said swiftly, pushing away the thought. "You haven't even seen my résumé and yet you are offering me the job on the spot."

"In my line of work, I've learned to read people well and quickly—and I already know you're right for the job." He gripped the edge of the counter and heaved himself up on it, crossing his legs so the heels of his climbing sneakers banged against the doors of the lower cabinet. "I can tell you're ambitious, intelligent, and sharp, and you know your business inside and out. You're also willing to take risks—otherwise you wouldn't be standing in an empty winery with a strange rock-climber who claims he owns the place." He peered at her more closely. "Yet there's a cautious side to you, isn't there, Amanda? A part of you that's wary, suspicious, a little frightened of the unknown—"

"How very Californian, Mr. Kane. What's next? Tarot cards?" She was uncomfortable with how close he was to the mark. "Did you consult an astrologer today to see if the moon was in the right house for hiring?"

"Nothing so unscientific." He grinned that baseball-player grin. "But I will admit, I cheated a little. I know a few things about you."

She crossed her arms in front of her. "Like what?"

"You won a gold medal last year, at the California State Fair."

It was the crown jewel on her résumé, for the wine-tasting competition at the California State Fair was one of the biggest competitions of the year.

"That's what the public relations firm told me when they mentioned your name."

She lifted a brow in surprise. "You've bent over backward to keep your identity a secret. What are you doing talking to a PR firm?"

"Unfortunately, the secrecy, and my privacy, will soon go out the window." He grimaced. "I had to hire a PR firm to launch this winery. Apparently, promotion is everything when it comes to selling the stuff to the restaurateurs and distributors in the industry."

She nodded. That was another reason why Mr. Brunichelli got out of the business and started selling his grapes.

"I knew I had to hire a winemaker within a week, and the firm suggested a number of qualified candidates." He picked up his beer beside him and toyed with the wet bottle. "I recognized your name because Miguel mentioned you, too. Before I knew I was going to put this winery on line, Miguel wanted to sell you this year's harvest. When I asked him why, he said you knew these vineyards better than any other winemaker in the valley."

Amanda tugged absently on the stem of her sunglasses. A PR firm and a single vineyardist were not the two best sources for information on winemakers, and she couldn't help suspecting that there was more to this than he was telling her.

"I must admit," he said, taking another sip of beer, "you're younger than I expected."

She tilted her chin, defensively. "I'm thirty years old—"

"And prime vintage," he interrupted, "if the old adage about wine and women is true."

"Then why," she said, her voice shaky, trying to ignore his double-edged comment, "haven't you offered the job to someone with more experience?"

"How do you know I haven't?"

"Because there isn't a winemaker in all of Napa who wouldn't snap up this offer in a minute."

"Are you hesitating, Amanda?"

"I'm *investigating*," she corrected. "There's a difference."

"Ah, yes, the consummate scientist." He shrugged his broad shoulders. "I'll tell you why I haven't offered the job to someone else. I don't want some winemaker who is set in his ways bulldozing in here and doing things the same way they've been done since Prohibition. I want someone who can adapt, who is willing to listen to what I want, yet still hold her own."

"You want someone you can mold."

"I want someone intelligent. I want someone who has enough experience for my needs, but is still open enough to learn. Someone innovative and flexible."

"All those requirements could be fulfilled by any eager young winemaker in Napa."

"I'm getting the feeling you don't think you can handle the job, Amanda."

"Of course I can handle the job." She ran a hand over her hair, tucking a few loose strands behind her ears. "I have no intention of being an assistant winemaker for the rest of my life—"

"Then why are you hesitating?" He tipped the mouth of the frosty beer toward her. "You *do* think you can hold your own with me, don't you, Amanda?"

"Of course I can."

She forced herself to meet his sultry gaze. If this conversation was any indication of what their working relationship might be like, she wasn't sure she could hold her own with him at all. And that, really, was the whole problem. Working with a man she was so physically attracted to was *not* the thing to do. It was a dangerous situation, like mixing hydrogen and oxygen and waiting for a spark.

But Lord, she wanted this job. At this moment, her head was as full of possibilities as her blood was full of hormones—and she was beginning to wonder if those rampaging little buggers were somehow affecting her good judgment. She still couldn't believe this brawny hunk of a man was offering her the position of a life-time—and it had nothing to do with the bedroom.

Garrick took a long draught of the beer, his eyes narrowing into slits as he watched her over the bottle. "This is far too spontaneous for you, isn't it?"

"Oh, no," she said drily. "Just yesterday another spandex-clad rock-climber asked me to take over his winery. You guys are a dime a dozen."

"Spontaneity is a good thing, you know." His voice had lowered to a dangerous huskiness. "Life gets boring unless you're thrown off kilter every once in a while."

"Around here we prefer the ground good and stable beneath our feet."

"Everyone needs a little jolt now and then," he persisted. "It forces you to remember how precious life is—and how rare certain opportunities are."

Something swift and silvery flickered in his eyes, as fleeting as the sight of a sleek, fast-moving fish in a deep pool of murky water. It was pain, deep and sharp—but before she could really see it, it was gone, submerged beneath one of his wry smiles.

"There's another reason why I want to hire you, Amanda."

She looked at him expectantly, searching for that glimmer again, wondering if she had seen it at all.

"You're a woman."

She started, then lifted a brow. "You noticed."

"Amanda, only a vegetable wouldn't."

She frowned. She had faced a lot of different attitudes from men during her years in the business. A few male colleagues—mostly younger men—treated her as an equal. Most men treated a female with a brain as some sort of strange, mutant creature—they respected her, but it took a lot longer to gain that respect. Others went out of their way to ignore her altogether. Then there were the few men who figured her only reason for being in the business was to seduce every male with whom she worked.

She wondered which category Garrick Kane fell into. "I prefer the men I work with to ignore the fact that I'm a woman," she said, "and look upon me as just another colleague."

"You expect a lot out of your associates."

"I expect to be treated like anyone else in the business, Mr. Kane." She crossed her arms over her chest protectively. "Now, tell me—what difference does it make that I'm a woman?"

He shrugged. "Call it crazy, but I think a woman would know more about the subtleties of wine than a man."

"That's not a very scientific observation. Most winemakers are men. I'm the exception to the rule."

"I'm not a scientist. I'm a businessman, and I've made my living on gut instinct." He leapt off the counter and walked toward her. He leaned close to her, so close she could see the individual bristles of his stubble, so close, she could smell the yeasty scent of beer on his lips. "You're right for the job, Amanda. I know it, *here.*"

He placed his hand just at the point where the spandex gave way to a stretch of bare chest. She stared at his hand, saw the grit beneath his fingernails, the streaks of soil and sweat, and the whorls of dark hair. It was a man's hand, hard and rough, and she wondered what it would feel like on her bare skin.

It was a completely inappropriate thought—disturbing and vivid. Her head was full of them today. It didn't help that she and Garrick stood too close for comfort, close enough to breathe the same air, to exchange the heat of their bodies, far too close for a professional relationship. She didn't know whether she was responding to his raw animal magnetism, or if her excitement was from the prospect of controlling a whole winery. She had to stop thinking like this. He was a business associate, the owner of a competing winery—but worse than that, if she took the job, he would be her *boss*.

This interview had simply started off on the wrong foot, she told herself. There was no reason to believe she couldn't eventually extinguish Garrick Kane's potent attraction if she became his employee. In the past, she had always managed to keep male colleagues at arm's length. A week or two of icy behavior, a few sharp, candid statements, and the men backed away.

Then she realized that, in her mind, she had already accepted the position.

"Miguel tells me the harvest begins soon." His gaze leveled with hers. "I need a decision today, before you leave. The offer won't be available tomorrow."

She told herself she had to look at the cellar first. She had to walk through the vineyards and test the grapes. She had to find out what he wanted out of a Cedar Ridge wine, she had to make sure he had the funds to keep the winery afloat for a few years until their first vintage went out. She couldn't just leave a prestigious position at Windsor to accept his outrageous, unexpected offer without analyzing every possible angle first.

She felt like she had just stepped off a cliff and now hung, weightless, in midair.

"Congratulations, Mr. Kane." She thrust out her hand. "You've just hired yourself a winemaker."

*   *   *

Garrick leaned against the doorjamb, swinging a ring of keys in his hand, watching the bewitching twitch of Amanda's slim hips as she strode across the dusty driveway to her blue pickup. The sun reflected off her smooth cap of ice-blond hair, and he found himself wondering what it would look like spread like flax across his bedpillow.

He shifted his weight as the spandex stretched uncomfortably across his loins. He didn't have to force those thoughts down anymore, now that she was safely ensconced in her truck and backing out of the driveway. Since the moment he had laid eyes on Amanda Karlson, standing like a Nordic goddess at the base of that cliff, he had fought a losing battle to keep his libido in check. Hell, he couldn't help it—no red-blooded man could. He could more easily imagine her clad in a little black dress, with those long, long legs encased in seamed hose, leaning on the bar of some posh New York nightclub or draped across the bow of a yacht with a wine spritzer in her hand than buried in a damp, dark cellar peering at round-bottom flasks.

The PR firm certainly would have nothing to complain about. Amanda fit all their specifications. They wanted him to hire a winemaker who would fit the "image" they intended to build for Cedar Ridge, someone who could provide an eye-catching "hook" in the press releases to wine distributors and dealers and restaurateurs to distinguish Cedar Ridge from the hundreds of other small wineries in the industry. Garrick had taken their list of suggested applicants, stuffed it in his pocket, and then told the PR firm that he didn't invest several million dollars in a winery to head it with someone who was all glitter and no substance. First and foremost, Garrick wanted a winemaker who could make wine.

Yet he ended up hiring exactly what the PR firm wanted—the sexiest female winemaker in Napa Valley.

He caught the twirling key ring in one hand and curled his fingers over the row of keys, letting the uneven edges dig into his palm. Before today, he had been sure such a creature as Amanda didn't exist—beautiful women just didn't become chemists. But she was a chemist, all right, from the sleek, neat little green suit right down to her sensible low-heeled shoes. He had interviewed her first because her name happened to be on the PR firm's list and Miguel had highly recommended her, and that was as good a place as any to start. After five minutes of talking with her, he knew she fit his requirements. She was intelligent, logical, insisting on facts before coming to a decision. His gut instinct told him she was perfect for the job, and the more he talked with her, the more convinced he became. When he had taken her around to the cluttered cellar, she had known the names and uses of every powder and liquid stored in an old fireproof cabinet, the purpose of every rusting piece of equipment lying about on the tables, the national origin of every oak barrel, and she had listed everything she would need to have the winery ready for the upcoming harvest—even recommending vendors and approximate prices.

He grinned as he remembered the stunned-rabbit look in her clear green eyes when he handed her a blank check. The lady wasn't used to surprises. A little bit of that slick poise shattered every time he said something to her that wasn't quite what she expected. He liked it. He intended to keep her off balance—and, if this relationship developed the way he wanted it to, he fully intended to keep her off her feet.

Amanda Karlson. He pushed away from the doorjamb and watched her pickup disappear down the steep road to the valley. He hadn't been this attracted to a woman for a very long time. Hell, he hadn't been this excited in years about anything that wasn't a granite cliff. There was something about her . . . She talked all business, but those full lips hinted at nothing but pleasure. She sparked something in him, something that had lain dormant for a long, long time. He wanted to burrow deep beneath the layers of her reserve, find the passionate woman he suspected lived beneath all that neatness and polish.

Kane, it's been too long. He jingled the keys in his hand and walked around the veranda to the other side of the house. It must be a delayed reaction to spending two months camping and climbing in Yosemite, he decided. He was acting like a wild mountain man laying his eyes on a woman for the first time in years. He'd best temper his enthusiasm before he saw her again or else he'd find himself tackling the lovely Amanda Karlson with as much finesse as a professional wrestler.

He descended the back stairs of the winery and walked to his car. Silence fell over the ravine, broken only by the musical chattering of the birds and the rustle of the heavy wind in the oak and madrone trees which edged the compound. The hot, sweet scent of ripening fruit rose like a cloud from the vineyards and permeated the yard. He scanned the vineyards, shimmering in the afternoon light. Lush with greenery, bowed with fruit, the verdant stalks stretched in wavering rows over the hillsides, reaching clear up to the rim of the long, narrow crater that formed the borders of Cedar Ridge.

This winery business was turning out to be a better idea than he had ever imagined. A friend in real estate had joined him in Yosemite last month and mentioned the opportunity over an open fire. Garrick had bought the house and vineyards, sight unseen—the first piece of real business he had done in well over a year. Usually he was more circumspect about large purchases of land, but he knew the vineyards would be a good investment, if nothing else. From the first moment he laid eyes on the redwood buildings and the hillsides green with vines, he felt as if he had finally come home.

A strange feeling for a boy from New York City. This verdant ravine in the Mayacamas mountains was a long way from the congested, gritty, throbbing pulse of Manhattan. But in a sense, he supposed he *had* come home. He and his older brother Dominick used to dream about spending their prime years on a winery in Bordeaux or California, once they made their fortunes. It had become a litany during the days they ran their Wall Street brokerage firm. Their fortunes had long been made, but somehow, until now, Garrick had never gotten around to fulfilling that particular dream.

And now Dominick wasn't around to enjoy it.

Suddenly, the silence of the ravine was interrupted by the wheezing and coughing of an ancient vehicle as it clambered up the slope into the driveway. Garrick swung his gym bag over his shoulder and turned around to see Miguel thrust his hand out the window of the truck in greeting. Garrick stayed well away from the churning cloud of dust until Miguel pulled to a stop in back of the main house.

Miguel jumped out of the driver's side, his bare

shoulders as dark as oiled cherrywood. *"Buenos días,* Señor Kane. Late in the day to start a climb."

"I've already finished." Garrick grimaced as he approached the rusted truck, the words "Cedar Ridge Winery" in faded red paint on the door. "When are you going to buy a new truck for the winery, Miguel? I gave you a check a week ago."

"It's unlucky to buy a new car during the harvest. You never know what could go wrong." Miguel shrugged a purely Latin shrug. "I'll buy it after the fruit is in."

"That thing looks like it couldn't pull a wheelbarrow, never mind a trailer full of grapes."

"This truck has seen twenty harvests," Miguel said, patting the rim of the flatbed as if it were the rump of a loyal horse. "It'll make it through another."

"Well, at least it won't have to travel far from the winery." Garrick adjusted the strap on his bag so it wouldn't dig into his shoulder. "I've decided not to sell the grapes this year. We're crushing them here. I just hired Amanda Karlson as the winemaker."

Miguel's black eyes widened. "I thought I passed her pickup on the way up. She's leaving Windsor?"

"Yes. She'll be coming here in the evenings for the rest of the week to set things up." Garrick remembered the stubborn set of her mouth as she insisted on staying at Windsor until the end of the week. Though he wanted her to start here immediately, he liked that kind of loyalty in an employee, and in a woman. "She starts full-time on Monday."

Miguel lifted his face to the sky, closed his dark eyes, and whispered something swift and thankful in Spanish. Then he planted his hands on his lean hips and grinned at Garrick. "If I had known you were going to hire *her*, I'd have worked for you for free."

"I'll keep that in mind when you ask for a raise."

"Amanda Karlson. Working *here*. She'll sure pretty up the place."

"I've got some business in San Francisco the rest of the week," Garrick said abruptly. "Give Amanda access to the cellar, the house, the vineyards—any place she wants to go."

"My pleasure." Miguel shook his head and blew air out between his lips. "Wait until you see her in those cut-offs she wears when she's testing the grapes."

"So you've told me."

"She's got legs right up to her neck, and those shorts hug her like a lover . . ."

Garrick's eyes narrowed on the vineyardist as Miguel began waxing rhapsodic about Amanda's physical virtues. Miguel hadn't hidden his interest in Amanda when Garrick had originally asked about her—in fact, Garrick encouraged Miguel to tell him every detail about the woman and then dismissed his praises as Latin effusiveness—but now that he had met her, Garrick was strangely reluctant to engage in male banter about her assets. He kept seeing Amanda standing in the kitchen, her back growing straighter and straighter every time he made a comment about her striking looks.

"She's a fellow employee," Garrick said suddenly, turning and heading toward the winery. "Unless you want trouble, don't talk like that around her."

"You crazy?" Miguel shook his head. "She'd stab me with her refractometer."

"Remember that. She's too good a winemaker and I don't want to lose her before she's even begun."

"You don't have to worry about me, Señor Kane."

Miguel's eyes glittered. "I'll be the perfect gentleman."

Garrick grunted and closed the door behind him harder than it needed to be closed. Miguel was a good-looking young buck—strong, brown as a berry, with the kind of swashbuckling pirate type of looks that women fell for in droves. Garrick knew that Miguel had been trying to win Amanda over for years, but seeing a woman once in a while was different from working with her every day. He wished he didn't have to leave Cedar Ridge and go to San Francisco for the rest of the week. The PR firm he had hired to launch this winery had insisted on two days of intense strategy talks to hammer out a campaign for the fall season. But suddenly, he didn't want to leave Amanda alone in this winery with Miguel.

And he knew why: If Amanda Karlson was going to fall for anyone in this winery, Garrick wanted to make damn sure it was *him*.

THREE

"Just listen, Amanda. Just listen!"

Maggie Johnson flopped down in a director's chair. Flat on her back on the wine-cellar floor, Amanda frowned at her friend and doggedly adjusted one of the valves on a fermentation tank. Perhaps it hadn't been a good idea to invite Maggie up to Cedar Ridge to help her clean out the wine cellar. Although Maggie was one of the best lab technicians at Windsor, she hadn't done anything but gossip since the moment she arrived.

"It's Sadie Cello's column, in the latest issue of the *Napa Weekly*." Maggie rustled the papers and lifted them to the light streaming in through the cellar's single window. " 'A little bird has been whispering in Sadie's ear, dear readers. Rumor has it that Miss Amanda Karlson, assistant winemaker at the Windsor Winery, has abruptly left her position to head the cellars of another winery—no less than Cedar Ridge, brought back from the dead by some mystery buyer. Keep twittering, birdies, keep twittering! Soon, soon, we'll know the identity of that secret buyer!' "

"Hand me that wrench, Maggie."

Maggie popped her head up over the paper. "How can you think about wrenches at a time like this?"

"It's easy. Harvest is coming and I've got a fermentation tank with a faulty valve. Twelve oak barrels of three-year-old Cabernet need to be bottled before the grapes come in, and—"

"You've made it to the big time! Can't you stop working for five minutes to enjoy it?"

"I wouldn't call a mention in Sadie Cello's column the 'big time.' " Amanda sat up and grabbed the wrench on the chair beside Maggie, then settled down to tighten a screw. "She's got more birds in her head than Napa has in the mountains."

"Well, she mentioned you in the same column as she mentioned André Bonchemin and a dozen winery owners." Maggie dug her sneakered foot into the canvas chair. "Where is that mystery buyer, anyway?" she muttered, peering out the window. "It looks like no one has lived in this place for years."

"So that's why you agreed to drag yourself up here on a Saturday afternoon. Just to snoop, hmm?"

Maggie shrugged without shame. Her brown hair, completely unmanageable in the dry summer heat, frizzed out of the constraints of her haphazard ponytail. "I thought I might get a peek at the mystery man."

"Well, sorry to disappoint you, Maggie, but he hasn't been around all week."

Secretly, Amanda was glad Garrick Kane had disappeared for a while. It gave her time to think about their strange meeting and his unusual offer. After a few evenings working in this cellar, she had become more and more convinced that coming to Cedar Ridge had been the right career move. The equipment was primitive compared to Windsor's, but she had worked with less in the barn of her parents' farm. At Cedar Ridge, it would be *her* wine, and she would be free of all the bureaucratic restraints that had held her back at Windsor.

Her feelings were more jumbled when it came to Garrick Kane. She had picked apart their first and only conversation so thoroughly in her mind that it had lost all meaning. She had finally come to the conclusion that she had simply overreacted to the presence of one of the most handsome men she had ever met. She hadn't had an intimate relationship with a man in a long time, so it was natural her body would respond to a well-muscled, half-naked rock-climber. Shortness of breath, sweaty palms, a racing pulse . . . they all were natural biological reactions to the company of an attractive male. She would simply have to control herself in front of him—no man wanted his employee drooling over him like an ice cream cone.

"Amanda, if you tighten that screw anymore, you're going to strip the threads."

Amanda stopped abruptly. She sat up and brushed the dirt off her cut-off jeans. "Well, that should just about do it."

"Are you sure there isn't something you want to share with me? You've been a little off center all week."

She tossed the wrench on the table next to some other tools. "You'd be 'off center,' too, if someone offered this position to you and you had barely two weeks to prepare." She flicked a switch on the tank and chose a temperature setting. "If this doesn't work, I'm going to have to order another tank and pray it's delivered in time."

"Just tell me what he looks like."

"Maggie, have you finished washing those flasks?"

"Listen, darling, you need the U.S. Army to clean this place up, not me."

Amanda peered around the cellar. The sink and counter area, which served as a lab, was cluttered with glassware, scales, a pH meter, and dozens and dozens of dirty beakers. A jumble of chemicals lay on the floor outside the fireproof cabinet, waiting for classification. Hoses ran all over the ground, some of them badly cracked and in need of replacement. For two days she had been inspecting the three large tanks which stood just in front of the entrance to the caves, a long room dug into the side of the cliff that held all the barrels used for aging wines. Her tools lay scattered all over the place.

She pushed behind her ear a strand of hair that kept falling out of her braid. "Listen, Maggie, a soldier can save his whole contingent with one act of bravery—"

"It'll take more than courage to face this." She wrinkled her freckled nose in distaste. "That owner must have made you an offer you couldn't refuse."

"It's not that bad." *And it's all mine.* "He gave me an open checkbook. I spent all week on the phone ordering new equipment."

"So he's rich." Maggie tilted her head, her hazel eyes glittering. "I suppose it's too much to ask that he'd be good looking, too?"

Amanda pushed a chair close to the tank and stood on it. Good-looking wasn't the half of it, but she certainly wasn't going to admit that to Maggie. "You're insatiable, aren't you?"

"Aren't you going to tell me anything? Some little morsel to tide me over until a little birdie twitters in Sadie's ear? A reward for washing all those beakers?"

"No—but you can hand me that long thermometer so I can see if this thing is working at all."

Maggie made an exaggerated growl of frustration, stood up from her comfortable curl on the director's chair, and handed her the thermometer. "You just wait until another lab tech falls head over heels in love with you. I swear I'll tell him that all that famed Karlson coolness is just a thin cover over a cauldron of pure lust—"

"Do that and I'll slash your tires."

"What's this I hear about a cauldron of pure lust?"

The thermometer almost slipped out of Amanda's fingers at the sound of Garrick's voice. She turned, nearly upsetting the chair beneath her in the process. Garrick closed the cellar door and strode across the room. He was fully dressed this time, but somehow, the charcoal-gray pinstripe suit didn't dull the raw force of his maleness. His tie had been pulled askew and the first button of his shirt was undone, and Amanda found herself thinking of a wildcat pulling and tugging at his collar.

"Oh, Amanda and I were just discussing her sex drive," Maggie said, stepping out in front of the newcomer. She thrust out her hand. "I'm Maggie Johnson. You must be the new owner of Cedar Ridge."

Garrick shook Maggie's hand, but didn't offer his name. His gaze slid over Amanda, and she became aware, for the first time, exactly how high the fray of her cut-offs ended on her thighs.

"It must have been an interesting conversation. I'm sorry I interrupted it."

"You didn't interrupt anything." Amanda climbed down from her perch upon the chair. "We were trying to fix this fermentation tank."

"On a Saturday?"

"Didn't you know you hired a workaholic?" Maggie's eyes sparkled. "She even conned me into coming up here to help her out."

"I didn't con you." Amanda placed the thermometer on the counter and wiped her hands with a rag. "You owe me, Maggie Johnson, for that day I did all your sugar readings while you went to a Grateful Dead concert."

"Oh, yeah."

Amanda frowned. Maggie was staring at Garrick as if he were a matinee idol. Amanda couldn't blame her. Somehow, the business suit only emphasized his raw masculinity. Still, Amanda couldn't help remembering his body bare but for a few strips of black spandex and a whole lot of sweat . . .

Easy, Amanda. Rope in those hormones. Remember, he's your boss.

"I tested the grapes yesterday," she said calmly, facing him as she leaned back on the counter. "They'll be ready for harvest in a week. I'm going to be working Saturdays and Sundays until we hire some cellar rats."

"I would think this cellar would draw rats in droves."

She blinked at him. This wasn't the first time he had misunderstood a simple phrase, something he should know if he was in the wine business. "A cellar rat is a low-paid drone willing to do grunt work to get his foot in the door of a winery."

"Oh." He shrugged. "Well, hire whoever you need."

"Five or six should be enough to get us through crush. I know some who might be available—"

"Call U. C. Davis," Maggie suggested inanely, for she knew Amanda knew exactly who to call. "There are always some students willing to work the harvest for pin money."

"How was your trip to San Francisco?" Amanda asked, ignoring Maggie's unnecessary advice. "Miguel made it sound like you wouldn't be back until Monday."

"I cut it short." Garrick glanced briefly at Maggie, then back to Amanda. "When you get a chance, Amanda, come up to the house and we'll talk about what you've been doing these past few days."

"Oh, don't delay business because of me!" Maggie clutched her enormous denim purse and pulled her fluorescent-pink sunglasses out of one of the innumerable pockets. "You two have things to discuss. I'll get out of your way."

Amanda started. "Maggie, you don't—"

"I've got to be going anyway." Maggie glanced at her watch so swiftly that she couldn't possibly have read the time. "I'm late for a lunch date."

"Have you eaten lunch yet, Amanda?"

Amanda looked at him. She felt dirty, disheveled, not utterly up to sitting in that sun-washed kitchen with him and sharing a meal. "No . . . but I haven't finished—"

"Finish it later." He headed toward the door. "I'll whip up something for us and we'll talk as we eat."

Then he was gone, leaving her alone with a tittering Maggie Johnson.

"My *God*, Amanda! No wonder you've been holding back on me!" She clutched her chest and faked a dramatic swoon. "That creature and Miguel Juarez on the same piece of land. You'd better get your blood pressure checked on a regular basis, girl."

"He's my boss, Mag—"

"You're talking to me, Amanda, not Sadie Cello. A blind man could see the lightning arcing between you two."

"I don't know what you're talking about."

"Honey, you're cold, but you're not dead." Maggie gave her an exaggerated look as she headed toward the door. "And I know you're not blind."

Amanda followed Maggie out of the cool, damp cellar into the heat of the afternoon sun. "All right, all right. So he's good-looking—"

"Amanda, Mel Gibson is good-looking. *That* man is Adonis in the flesh. And Adonis was staring at your legs."

Amanda pulled on the frayed edge of her shorts. "Now you're imagining things."

Maggie opened the door to her multicolored Volkswagen bug. "What did he say his name was?"

"He didn't."

"And obviously you're not telling." Maggie frowned in thought. "I know I've seen him somewhere."

"Probably in your dreams."

"Honey, I don't have that much imagination." Maggie turned the ignition and smiled wickedly. "Have a nice lunch. I want to hear all the scintillating details tonight."

"Try not to crash on the way down the hillside, Maggie," Amanda muttered. "Remember—you still owe me."

She walked across the driveway to the back of the main house, her sneakered feet dragging over the dry earth. Mentally, she listed all the things she would have to discuss with Garrick during lunch, enough to keep the conversation flowing for a solid hour. Everything would be fine, she told herself, as long as there were no long, uncomfortable pauses which they would feel obligated to fill with small talk about their personal lives.

With Garrick Kane, Amanda was determined to keep everything strictly business.

He was waiting in the kitchen, his suit jacket and tie flung haphazardly over the back of one of the chairs, the sleeves of his white shirt rolled up to his elbows. As she entered, he glanced at her over an egg mixture sizzling in a frying pan. "I hope you like cheese omelets."

"Fine." She didn't add that she couldn't remember any man ever cooking anything for her. "Can I help you with anything?"

"This doesn't require a chemist's touch." He shook the pan. "I promise you a better meal another time. I haven't had a chance to shop this week."

Aha. Topic number one. She leaned back on the opposite counter, at a safe distance from Garrick's broad shoulders. "So, how was your trip to San Francisco?"

"Long." With a flip of his wrist, he folded the omelet and pressed it down with the spatula. "This PR firm has some elaborate plans to launch Cedar Ridge. They want me to attend every party held in Napa, and they want to hold an opening here in the middle of October."

"October?"

He slipped the first omelet on a plate. "Is that a problem?"

She thought of all the work that needed to be done

in the next two months. "Hopefully, the opening will take place during a pause in the harvest, right before the cabernet grapes ripen."

"Good." He poured more egg mixture into the frying pan and the scent of hot butter and melted cheese filled the kitchen. "The firm's planning lots of media coverage, and we'll be inviting every winery owner in the valley."

Amanda paled. She had heard about the bashes held in the winery community—elaborate, glittering affairs that were always written up ad nauseam in Maggie's gossip sheets. She had never been invited to them—until now, she hadn't been in the same class. This was just another indication of how far she'd advanced in just a matter of days.

Then she realized that she would probably be attending the galas as Garrick's escort. Eating with him, drinking with him. Perhaps even dancing with him. Her heart jumped a little at the prospect.

Garrick was suddenly in front of her, handing her the plate with the first steaming omelet. "Are you pale with hunger or pale with fright?"

"Neither." She took the plate and said the first thing that popped into her mind. "I don't know what I'm going to wear."

His gaze wandered all over her, from her messy braid down to the frayed edge of her faded cut-offs. "What you're wearing looks fine to me."

Her heart gave a dangerous little leap. Pushing away from the counter, she walked to the white pine table and placed the plate on it harder than she intended. "Shorts aren't appropriate for these bashes. I'll obviously have to do some clothes shopping before October.'' She wiped a strand of hair off her forehead and asked, "What do you have to drink?"

He returned to the stove to finish cooking the second omelet. "Help yourself to whatever is in the fridge. And get me a beer while you're there."

"You're going to have to stop drinking beer."

"I know." He grimaced, "The PR people harped on me about that all week."

"It's suicide to support the competition." She opened the fridge and pulled out a beer and a single can of cola that stood abandoned in the back. Then she remembered topic number two. "We could have wine with lunch."

"I don't have any."

"Oh, yes, you do." She put the beverages back, closed the fridge with a hip, and headed out of the kitchen. "The day before yesterday I found twelve oak barrels of Cabernet aging in the caves. It was old Mr. Brunichelli's last batch. I'll go draw some off—"

"Amanda." He gestured to the frying pan as she stopped near the door. "Wine and omelets don't go well together."

"Myth," she argued. "Wine goes with anything. And you have to taste this Cabernet. It's good enough to serve at the Cedar Ridge opening."

"Fine. I'll trust your judgment. In the meantime, I'll drink beer."

"You should at least taste it—"

"Listen, Amanda, it's time for my confession." He finished his omelet and slid it on a plate. "I have the taste buds of a Neanderthal. All I know about wine is that the good stuff comes with a cork." He pulled the cola and the beer out of the fridge, lifting the beer toward her. "Now if we were tasting some of this, I could tell you the city in which it was brewed within ten square miles. But wine— Sorry. That's why I hired you. Come eat before your omelet gets cold.''

Amanda wandered back to the kitchen table, stunned, watching him burrow in a drawer for forks and knives. The suspicions that had been budding in her mind for days burst into full bloom.

She sank into a chair. ''This is the first winery you've ever owned, isn't it?''

''First and only.'' He handed her a fork and a knife and sat next to her at the oval table. He cut into the omelet and lifted a bite, dripping with cheese, to his mouth. ''I'm part owner of a company that makes pens that light up in the dark, too, but you don't see me bringing them to business meetings.''

Amanda suppressed a groan. A *dilettante.* She wondered if he realized how much work went into running a winery, if he realized that it usually took four or five years before an owner ever saw a dime of profit—if he saw any profit at all. She wondered how long it would take before he grew bored with this venture, sold off the land at a profit, and moved on to bigger and better things.

Suddenly, she doubted her decision to leave Windsor and come here.

''Hey, I'm not the best cook in the world, but the omelet can't be that bad.''

She looked up. She realized she hadn't touched her food yet. She picked up her fork and toyed with the edge of the omelet. ''Did you know that most wineries this size in Napa are on the verge of bankruptcy?''

He took another bite and shrugged. ''Is that why I got this land at such a good price?''

She rested her forehead on one hand as she twirled her fork in some cheese. "How many years will you run the winery before you get restless and go back to making pens that glow in the dark?"

"It's not that easy. I bought this place not just as a winery but as a home. I intend to stay here a good long time—and keep the Cedar Ridge Winery running at the same time. Is that what you're worried about?"

"I took a big risk leaving Windsor."

"And now you're thinking it's a mistake?" His fork clattered on his plate and he pushed it aside. "It wasn't. I've never run a winery before—so I did what any exec would do. I hired help. First Miguel, then a PR firm, and now I've hired you." He leaned toward her, and his voice lowered to a husky roughness. "I trust your abilities implicitly, Amanda Karlson."

He did. She saw it in his eyes. He was handing her total control of the wine cellars, without question and without hesitation. There were few owners who would give up so much control to their employee. Furthermore, there was something in his expression, something determined and sure and confident. Somehow, she believed he would stay at Cedar Ridge.

Then he touched her and all thoughts of winemaking flew out of her head. It was a gentle touch, like the brush of a feather against her cheek, and it took her so much by surprise that she froze, like a deer facing a car's oncoming headlights.

Men in the business tried to touch her all the time. They tried to pat her bottom, to clutch her bare knee, or to brush "innocently" against her breast. Whenever it happened, she pushed them away, firmly and decisively, glaring at them so they knew she was onto them. But this was different. This was no sexual advance.

Garrick was touching her face, gently, reverently. There was magic in his fingers. A current passed between them, heavy and languid, igniting the air around them with sparks.

For a moment she sat, silent, food forgotten, their only contact the brush of his hand against her cheek and the meeting of their gazes. Her heart thumped, hard, again, then found a new tempo. He found a tendril of moonlit-colored hair lying against her neck and he wound it around his fingers, staring in silence at the silvery ringlet.

Her voice came out as an uneven whisper. "Mr. Kane—"

"Garrick." He let the tendril unwind and then he rubbed the edge of her jaw. "It's not so tough a name, Amanda. I'd like to hear it on your lips."

She started to say it, but his name lodged in her throat. Something was happening here, in the close confines of this sun-washed kitchen, something she didn't completely understand. One part of her consciousness heard the muted chirping of a bird singing outside the kitchen window. Another part of her smelled the tart melted cheese rising from her plate. But all this was peripheral, for every nerve ending on her body was tuned on Garrick, like a million tiny magnetic needles all pointed north.

"Come horseback riding with me."

She blinked, heavily, for she felt like she was moving through water. "Horseback riding?"

"Yes." His chair squeaked against the linoleum as he leaned closer to her. "I found a place in the valley that rents horses by the hour. We could ride into the western hills."

It sounded marvelous, mounting a steed and riding

into the forests with him. They could go somewhere private, somewhere quiet, where he could lift her off her horse with his bare, strong hands and lay her down on the grass . . .

She stiffened. She closed her eyes, breaking contact with his mesmerizing gaze. This was pure madness. She was doing exactly what she had sworn not to do—succumbing to the powerful force of Garrick's personality.

He dropped his hand from her cheek. "Well, Amanda? Is it yes or no?"

She blinked her eyes open again. His collar was open at the throat, showing a few whorls of dark hair. She leaned far back in the chair to put the maximum distance between them. "It's no," she said, tugging on the fringe of her shorts. "I've got too much work to do. Besides, it's not a good idea—"

"It's a great idea, and you shouldn't be working on Saturdays." He smiled that lazy, baseball-player grin. "I want to get to know you better—"

"That's exactly why it's not a good idea." She stood up abruptly, pushing away the cold, untouched omelet. She couldn't fight against that blinding smile. "Now, if you'll excuse me, I've got to check on that fermentation tank."

He stood up and blocked her retreat, and she nearly slammed into that wide, glorious chest. She got a faint whiff of some spicy, elegant cologne—enough to send her reeling away so that she stumbled back against her chair.

"You've been working all week at Windsor and every night here," he argued, not moving away. "The tank will be there tomorrow. You need some R&R."

She looked up at him, stiffening her spine, drawing

herself up to her full five feet eight inches. He stood just under six feet, and she found herself thinking that the difference in height was perfect for dancing . . . or kissing.

Unconsciously, her gaze fell to his lips, then slipped back up to his eyes. Eyes that blazed with a sudden heat.

"Hell, Amanda." He took her face in his hands. "You know it's going to happen sooner or later."

Then his mouth was on hers. Her body jolted as if she had touched a live wire with wet hands. His fingers curled into her hair. She pressed her palms flat against his chest, scraping the cool, crisp cotton of his shirt and feeling the heat and hardness of his body beneath. She tilted her head, unconsciously accommodating him, pressing her nose deep into his bristled cheek. The woodsy scent of his cologne muddled her senses and nudged awake long-denied urges. It was just his lips against hers—just two organs of tender flesh pressing against one another, moist and hot—yet deep inside her, something primitive, something uncontrollable, threatened to erupt.

The feeling filled her with terror.

"Stop." She twisted away, still pressing her fingers against his chest. "*Stop*."

He did. She felt the beat of his heart against her palms, and the vibration of his voice as he made a low, rumbling, uninterpretable noise. His hands slipped down to her shoulders and he held her still. "What is it?" His voice was rough and impatient against her ear. "Is there another man?"

"No."

"Good." He flexed his fingers over her arms. "You

know as well as I that something has been boiling between us since the first time we saw each other—"

"I don't know what you're talking about."

He touched her chin and forced her to look up at him. She blinked, naked and vulnerable under his gaze. His fingers slipped down to where a pulse fluttered like a butterfly's wings in her throat. "Yes, you do, Amanda."

"Why are you doing this?" She tried valiantly to take control of her treacherous body. "Is this a job requirement that I know nothing about?"

"This has nothing to do with your job." His fingers gentled on her arms. "This took me by surprise, too. One hell of a pleasant surprise."

She broke away from him and stepped back, colliding with the chair. She clutched the back and curled her fingers over the wood. Alarms rang in her head, loud and raucous. This was exactly what she was trying to avoid—exactly the situation she swore she would never get herself into. Exactly the situation she had feared since the moment she agreed to work for Garrick Kane.

He stood with his hands on his hips, his eyes smoky and dark blue, watching her like a predatory hawk. He wanted her. She felt his desire like a third presence in the room—tangible, palpable—and it didn't help that she felt like spreading her arms and letting him touch her in all the ways only a man could touch a woman. She had admitted the pure sexual desire on her part, but she hadn't counted on his returning it a thousandfold—and she hadn't counted on feeling so out of control, so swept away by such a raw, undiluted, hungry emotion.

The situation was impossible. Long ago, she had

made it an iron-clad rule never to mix business with pleasure. It was just common sense for most people, but for a female winemaker in a male-dominated industry, it was pure survival.

She took a deep breath and glanced out the window, narrowing her eyes at a few birds pecking in the shade. One of them flew off, and she was struck with terror as she imagined the bird flying directly to Sadie Cello's door. Amanda suppressed a groan. She could just imagine what Sadie Cello would do if she discovered that Amanda Karlson, recently of the Windsor Winery, was found playing tonsil hockey with the tall, muscular owner of Cedar Ridge—*her new employer*. Amanda would be in every issue of the *Napa Weekly* until some other tart's underwear was found in the wrong bed. She could imagine the raised eyebrows, the secret, knowing nods. Now all those inquiring minds would "know" how she got the job as winemaster at Cedar Ridge. How else would a young, relatively inexperienced woman land such a fine position, except on her back? A scandal like that could destroy her career forever in this small, gossipy place.

And her career was everything. Her career was stability and safety—security in an insecure world. From an early age she had been determined never to depend—financially or emotionally—on anyone but herself. She wouldn't risk her career for anything—not even for a fling with the most handsome man she had ever known.

"This shouldn't have happened." She smoothed her damp palms over her hips and stepped behind the chair to bring some space between her and Garrick. "You're my employer."

"I'm also a single adult male who's very interested in a certain single adult female—"

"I never get involved with anyone in the business."

"There's always a first time."

"You're new to this place," she argued, crossing her arms over her chest. "You don't know how small the Napa community is, how little it would take for people to start whispering about us."

"Is that what you're worried about? Gossip?"

"Isn't that enough?" She tilted her chin. "I've been fighting for respect in this profession since I took my first course in winemaking—"

"Listen, Amanda, I'm not saying—"

"I've worked hard to build a reputation as a damn good winemaker," she interrupted, all her pent-up frustration flooding to the surface. Men were always blind to double standards. "You wouldn't have heard of me if I hadn't. But I could lose that fine reputation in a millisecond, with one choice tidbit of gossip. I'm not going to let my career be ruined by malicious chatter or stained by hints of impropriety."

He lifted his hands to his hips, then let his gaze slip over her, slowly, intimately. "No matter what you do, people are going to talk."

"Not if there's nothing to talk about."

"They're going to take one long look at you, know that I'm a single, red-blooded man, and they're going to draw their own conclusions." He shook his head. "And there's not a damn thing you can do about it."

Her eyes flared. "We'll just have to fight that every step of the way, won't we, Mr. Kane?"

"Frankly," he murmured, "I'd rather ride with the rapids than swim against the current."

"Then we'll just have to set some ground rules."

Amanda pushed the chair into the table and faced him, fully, with nothing between them but her determination. "The first is—no fraternizing outside of business."

He rubbed the back of his neck with his hand. "I guess that means you don't want to go horseback riding."

"The second is . . ." She flushed as she looked him straight in the eye. "No more kissing. On or off the job."

"Is *that* what you call that chemistry experiment that almost bubbled out of control?"

"I'm quite serious." She dug her fingernails into her arm, hoping the pain would somehow stem the rise of her involuntary goosebumps. "If you don't agree to the rules, then I'm going to have to reconsider my position here. It's not too late for me to return to Windsor and for you to find another winemaker."

He searched her level gaze. Finally, he said, "I don't want to lose a fine winemaker."

"Good. I'm glad that's settled. Now, if you'll excuse me . . ." She slipped by him as he stepped aside, "I've got work to do in the wine cellar."

Mindlessly, Amanda found her way out of the house into the bright, blinding sun. She paused on the veranda and clutched a thick, woody wisteria vine that wound its way over the trellis that shaded the veranda. She waited for her senses to stop swirling and settle. A lump rose to her throat, and she felt an unexpected bite of tears at the back of her eyes.

She was being foolish. She had closed the door on a romantic possibility. It wasn't the first time she had shut down her emotions for the sake of her future, and it surely wouldn't be the last. She wondered why this time it left such a bitter taste in her mouth.

She took a deep breath and walked across the drive to the wine cellar. There was no use dwelling on it. The lines had been drawn. Her career, her security, her hard-earned peace of mind—none of these things were in danger anymore.

And that was all that really mattered.

FOUR

"Garrick, I didn't give your phone number to *anyone*." The woman on the other end of the phone sighed loudly in Garrick's ear. "Reporters can be very resourceful. Maybe this one has a friend in the phone company—I don't know. But, Garrick dear—however he *did* get your number, you should be taking his calls, anyway."

Garrick frowned into the phone and twirled a bright-green glow-in-the-dark pen between his fingers. "It's not worth my time. If it were, your firm would have contacted him already."

"There's no such thing as bad publicity, especially bad *free* publicity." Shelley Weintraub raised her voice, singsong, which reminded Garrick of a third-grade teacher trying to cajole a student into behaving. "You've got to stop being a hermit, Garrick. You own a winery now."

"If he calls again, I'll think about it."

"Do that. And don't forget the *Winery* interview tomorrow."

61

Garrick's mind went blank. He rolled his forearm over his desk to clear his monthly calendar of debris.

"You forgot, didn't you?" Shelley released an exaggerated groan. "You're a promoter's nightmare, Garrick Kane. *Winery* is *the* journal to be seen in, and you've forgotten the appointment as if it were a trip to the dentist."

"I've got it written down right here."

"Underneath all your rock-climbing journals and a pile of fluorescent pens."

Garrick winced as he realized how close she had come to the truth.

"I suppose you haven't told the new winemaker yet, have you?"

He glanced out the window of his office, which faced the vineyards. From his vantage point he could see Amanda's straw hat and Miguel's dark head poking above the vines. "She'll be here." *Hell, she's been here every day for nearly two weeks.*

"Garrick, they're bringing a photographer. Women have to prepare for these things. Hair, nails, makeup. She's got to be dressed for it—no lab coats and goggles, none of that dry scientist stuff. Remember, image—"

"—Is everything. You're becoming predictable, Shelley.

"Ten A.M. sharp, Kane. And do me a favor. Don't be clinging to some cliff face when they arrive, okay?"

Garrick grunted, snapped down the antenna of the portable phone, and tossed it on the cluttered desk. He rubbed his aching ear with the heel of his hand. He had been on the phone all morning, mostly to New York City, and his desk was scattered with a dozen scribbled notes. He had spent a good two hours listening to the harried, breathless voice of his Wall Street

broker, writing down the blunt, meticulous instructions
of his Madison Avenue lawyer as the attorney's ticker
counted off quarter hours in the background and catching up with all his other business associates in Manhattan. His lungs ached for a cigarette—a sure sign that it
was time to stop working.

He rose from his leather chair, walked to the window, and gazed over the shimmering vineyards. Talking to New York always made him restless and anxious,
as if he were still there, steeped neck-deep in the madness. These days, all he could remember of his old
lifestyle was a blur of numbers, a thousand jerky cab
rides through potholed streets, the stench of smoke and
Scotch and rich French sauces consumed in oak-paneled
rooms. He remembered the quick decisions in which
millions were made or lost, and then the euphoric celebration of victory, or the hazy solitude of defeat.

Lately, it felt like another life to him—someone
else's life—yet it had only been a year since he'd given
it up. He and Dominick, his brother and partner in their
company, Granite Investments, had once thrived on
pure adrenaline, but now just the thought of the big
city raised Garrick's blood pressure to an uneasy high.
His lust for the fast lane died the same day Dominick
died.

Garrick rubbed his hand over his unshaven chin and
watched Amanda's huge straw hat bob among the
vines. Amanda reminded him of Dominick. Both lived,
breathed, ate, and slept immersed in their work. Worka-
holicism obviously wasn't confined to the island limits
of Manhattan. It had been nearly two weeks since he
had hired Amanda, and she was always at the winery,
either directing the young, eager cellar rats she had
hired for the harvest, or talking on the phone with ven-

dors, or setting up new equipment, or supervising the bottling of the red wine she had found aging in the caves, or running through the vineyards with Miguel.

He leaned against the window frame and frowned. He wished she were simply trying to work off some pent-up frustration in the fields. Hell, *that* motivation he could understand. He had climbed the cliff every morning since they had shared that explosive kiss, trying to sweat off the memory. It hadn't worked. He wanted Amanda Karlson even more now that he had tasted the passion hidden beneath her calm. He had let his libido race far ahead of his common sense that day—but, hell, she had looked up at him with those big green eyes and he knew they had been sharing the same single thought. Now she held him back with both hands, forcing him to abide by her rules, but that was like trying to put a cork back in an open bottle of champagne. He knew, sooner or later, that cork was going to pop—explosively. It was up to him to make sure, next time, that she trusted him enough to let her passion flow.

He watched as she bent over a vine, her straw hat disappearing behind the greenery. Garrick's brows lowered over his eyes. Whatever else had happened between them—whatever else would happen between them in the future—he had no intention of watching her work herself to the bone. The symptoms were so familiar to him now. Some people chose the bottle. Others chose drugs. People like Amanda Karlson—and people like Dominick Kane—drowned their worries and their fears in their work.

Garrick turned on one heel and headed toward the door to his study. Unlike Dominick, Amanda was his employee. He could control her time—and it was time they both took a break.

An hour later, Garrick strode up the side of the hill, through a neat row of fragrant, heavily laden grape-vines, toward where Miguel stood in the sun. By the thrust of Miguel's bare brown chest and by his easy smile, Garrick knew Amanda must be nearby. He didn't spot her until he was practically upon her.

She was on her knees in the dirt. Garrick stopped in his tracks and drank in the vision of one long, shapely, gleaming leg, stretched out in his path for balance while she searched deep among the leaves for a clump of grapes. The pert curve of her breasts strained against the soiled cotton of her T-shirt. Through the thin mate-rial he could see she was wearing a bra—but there wasn't much to it but a wisp of lace. A bottle of sun-screen poked out of the back pocket of her legendary cut-offs.

Miguel met Garrick's gaze. The younger man grinned, rolled his eyes, and clutched his bare chest over his heart.

"They look perfect, Miguel." Amanda fell back on her heels, a cluster of gleaming green grapes hanging from one hand and a small, curved knife in the other. "Hand me the refractometer, will you? I'll bet they're twenty-one, maybe twenty-two degrees Brix." She looked up suddenly and started. "Oh! Hello. I didn't know you were here."

She looked like some sort of pagan tropical god-dess. The wide brim of the straw hat cast a rosy glow over her features. Three white stripes of sunblock protected her nose and the high curve of her cheeks just beneath her eyes. The bright sunlight, filtering through the mesh of verdant grape leaves, made her eyes look vividly green.

"I'll take that refract— That thing." Garrick held out his hand as Miguel pulled a black instrument about the length of a screwdriver out of his back pocket. "You won't be needing this for the next hour, Amanda."

"I certainly will!" She folded the blade into her knife against her hip, shoved the case into her front pocket, and struggled to her feet. "I haven't even begun testing the sugar on the opposite slopes—"

"The grapes will wait." He shoved the instrument into the front pocket of his own khaki walking shorts. "We have business to discuss."

"Couldn't that business wait until sundown?" She curled her fingers over the cluster of grapes. "Harvest begins the day after tomorrow and Miguel and I have a lot of work to do."

Garrick met Miguel's gaze. Garrick didn't like the gleam in Miguel's dark eyes, and he didn't like the way the vineyardist had been looking at Amanda. Garrick also didn't like the fact that Amanda had practically spent every day in this young, virile buck's presence— willingly—while she had gone out of her way to avoid him.

"Miguel would be more than happy to finish this up tomorrow." He let a thread of dare enter his voice. "Wouldn't you, Miguel?"

Miguel shrugged his brown shoulders and made an exaggerated yawn. "It's time for siesta, anyway."

Garrick shifted the weight of the small backpack he wore on his back, then headed down the row. He turned around to find her standing, staring at him, grapes in hand. "Come on, Amanda. Time's wasting."

She handed the grapes none too gently to Miguel, then followed. Garrick strode through the row until he came to a break in the long, horizontal wires that supported the new canes of the vinestalks. Then, without a word, he passed through the opening to the next higher row, waited until he saw her follow, then he cut through the successive rows, climbing higher and higher on the steep vineyard.

"Where in God's name are you going?" she exclaimed breathlessly when they had almost reached the upper rim of the vineyards. "I thought you wanted to talk business."

"We *are* going to talk business." He never slackened in his pace. "We're going to do it over lunch."

"I finished lunch a half hour ago. Miguel and I ate while we worked."

Garrick frowned. "I bet Miguel enjoyed that."

"And what," she said, grasping the foliage of a vine in one hand and pulling herself up the slope, "is that supposed to mean?"

"It means that Miguel takes a lurid interest in what's hidden beneath those cut-offs, Amanda." He turned and paused, watching her catch up. "Is he just a 'business associate,' too?"

She stopped. Her chin tilted defiantly. "Just like you, Mr. Kane. Just like you."

Garrick wasn't sure that was a good thing, for he had definite plans to change Amanda's mind about not mixing business with pleasure. He turned and headed back up the slope, releasing a small avalanche of pebbles with each step as they reached the rocky rim. They left the cooler confines of the vineyard, but he didn't stop. He headed still higher, over the edge of the hill, where the thin soil gave way in places to bare granite.

His goal was a small spot on the edge of the Cedar Ridge holdings, where a cluster of oak trees stood like sentinels on a level peak.

He reached it before she did. Swinging the loaded backpack off his shoulders, he pulled out an old red checkered tablecloth and spread it over the scraggly grass in the shade of one of the trees. He sat on the edge and pulled out two sourdough baguettes, some mushed Brie, and searched through the rest of the debris until he found a half dozen shiny red apples.

She approached the feast and looked down at him, frowning, her hands on her hips.

He held out a bottle of water. "Here. You look like you need it."

Wordlessly, she took the water, unscrewed the top, and lifted it to her lips. When she finished, she frowned down at him. "A rather unlikely spot for a business meeting, Mr. Kane."

He glanced over his shoulder, to the lush fields of Sonoma County spread below. In the distance, he could just barely make out the hazy silhouette of the San Francisco skyline. "I do my best work on heights."

She screwed the top back on the water. "I do mine in the vineyards or the lab."

"You do too much of it, too." He pulled out the last apple and tossed it toward the rest. "By the way, you should know that a reporter and a photographer from the magazine *Winery* are coming here tomorrow to interview us."

"*Winery*?!" she gasped. "They're coming *here*?"

"Ten A.M. sharp. The PR firm wants us dressed 'professionally,' whatever that means."

She sank down to her knees, tossed the bottled water on the cloth, and pulled her straw hat off her head.

"Do you realize that *Winery* is the biggest vintners' publication in the country?"

"Shelley mentioned that."

"You could have given me a few more days to prepare." She waved her hat in front of her face, sending tendrils of damp blond hair flying. "How long have you known?"

"The PR people reminded me this morning." He pulled six bottles of wine out of his backpack one by one and lined them up on the edge of the tablecloth. "I need your tongue, Amanda."

She jumped as if she had sat on a nest of wasps. "Excuse me?"

"I don't want to make a complete ass out of myself in front of this reporter." He pulled a corkscrew out of his pocket and dug the tip into the cork of the first bottle of wine. "You're going to teach me how to tell good wine from bad."

She stopped waving her hat. "All in one afternoon?"

"I was hoping you could do it in an hour."

She looked at him blankly. "There are people who spend a lifetime learning about wine—"

"I'm good at cramming." He fumbled with the corkscrew as bits of cork flaked off the top. "I learned Management Principles and Basics of Marketing both in one night. That's how I made it through business school."

"Don't—" She took the bottle and the corkscrew from his hand as more cork broke off. "That's a Gewurtztraminer."

"*Gesundheit.*"

Her full, sensuous lips twitched. "It's a sweet wine, from German grapes. You should open this last. Wines should be tasted from the driest to the sweetest."

"Ah, then you *will* turn this beer-drinking slob into a wine aficionado."

"I'm a chemist, not a magician," she said drily. "Chemists gave up trying to turn lead into gold centuries ago."

He grasped his heart and tumbled onto his back. "Ouch. Direct hit."

"But you are my boss, and I can't afford to have you serving generic jug wine to a couple of reporters from *Winery.*" She scanned the six bottles and the food scattered on the tablecloth. "You seem to have brought all the right equipment."

"The young lady at the store was very accommodating."

"I'm sure she was." She twisted one of the bottles to get a better look at the label. "Not a bad selection of wine, either."

"They all have corks." He lifted himself on his elbow, grinning as he tore an end off one of the sourdough baguettes. "And the prices vary from outrageous to obscene."

She rolled her eyes, but he saw a glimmer of pearly teeth. "I can't believe you know nothing about all this. You're a businessman. Haven't you ever taken clients out to a fancy restaurant and ordered wine?"

"That was Dominick's job." When she looked at him quizzically, he added, "My brother and business partner and overall man of good taste. He used to scan the wine lists, order some expensive bottle, and take care of all the folderol that went with tasting it. I usually passed and ordered a beer."

She handed him a bottle of red wine. "Why isn't *he* here, running the winery?"

"He's dead."

She blinked at him. She clasped the corkscrew between her hands and fiddled with the handle. "I'm sorry." She looked at him with serious green eyes. "I didn't realize—"

"Of course you didn't." Garrick twisted the bottle of red by the neck, wondering why he had told her such an intimate detail so soon and so suddenly. "It happened a little over a year ago. We used to talk about owning a winery when we were old and gray. His death made me think about doing it a hell of a lot sooner."

She nodded toward the fields of Sonoma. "Do you think he would have liked this place?"

"He would have loved it." Garrick lifted himself on one elbow, determined to sweep away the cloud he had cast over the moment. He had dragged Amanda away from the fields to relax her, not to burden her with his own painful memories. His eyes twinkled as he swept her with his gaze. "Dominick would have loved you, too. He had a weakness for blondes. He married two of them."

Her lips twisted in a wry smile. "I assume not at the same time?"

"Dominick was a hellion, but he wasn't a fool." He reached for the corkscrew. "And I've got a long way to go to match his expertise in winetasting—"

"Ah-ah." She yanked the corkscrew out of his reach. "Tasting comes later, Mr. Kane. Your brother could have told you that. Lesson number one is how to read the label."

The moment of solemnity passed. Amanda slipped into a smooth, lucid discourse about table wine. Garrick listened as she pointed out the differences between the shapes of the bottles, talked about the different grape varieties that grew in Napa and what kind of wine they made. The lady obviously knew her business inside and out, and when he mentioned it, she shrugged and leaned close to explain each line on the label of the bottle he held.

His throat went as dry as the Mojave Desert. The faint coconut scent of her sunscreen, warmed by the heat of her skin, filled his head. Vintage dates and grape varieties lost all meaning when a lock of her moonlight-colored hair innocently brushed his shoulder. She reached over and tilted the bottle back against his knee, so she could read the fine print at the bottom of the label. Her head was only a few inches from his chest, her hair a breath away from his mouth. He wanted to touch her, to wrap his fingers in the sleek silk of her hair, to bury his nose in the scented, vulnerable hollow where her neck met her shoulder. He didn't make a move. He tried to control his breathing. He tried closing his eyes, but then he could feel the heat and scent of her all the more strongly, so instead, he kept his gaze fixed on the vista of Sonoma County below. *Christ, Kane, pull yourself together.* He tried telling himself that she was just a woman, but the woman practically draped across his lap was Amanda Karlson, chemist, winemaker, whose kiss had all the power and intensity of a nuclear explosion. He had made the mistake of giving in to his urges once before. It had set his cause back weeks. He'd be a fool to make today a repeat performance.

But she felt so good, so close to him. . . . His gaze slid unwittingly away from the vista to the woman beside him. Her legs had browned slightly from days in the sun, and they gleamed with moisture and sunscreen. Her faded cut-offs ended in a frayed hem, and on her hip a slight cut showed more skin, a little higher on her smooth hip. It would be so easy to wrap one arm around her, to dig his fingers into her slim waist. If she lifted her head, she'd be leaning against his shoulder and he could tilt her chin up with one finger and coax all her secrets out with one gentle kiss . . .

"Amanda."

She stopped in the middle of explaining something, sat back, and looked at him. "What is it? Are you confused about the sulfites?"

"No." He grasped the bottle of wine more tightly in his lap. He had said her name almost as a plea, hoping she would move away before he touched her, and now that he had succeeded, he searched for an intelligent question.

"I'm going too fast, aren't I?" She brushed a lock of hair behind her ear. "It's always like that when I get warmed up to a subject—"

"No." His gaze fell upon the cheese, softening in the heat. "I was just wondering when we'd eat."

The white stripes of sunblock tilted over her cheeks. "I forgot that this is your lunch." She handed him the corkscrew. "We'll eat something between the wines to clear our palates."

He took the corkscrew and dug it into the cork. He was beginning to wish Cedar Ridge distilled whiskey. He needed a swig of something strong—immediately.

"Easy, easy." Her hands covered his. "It's a cork, not a piece of granite." She took the corkscrew and bottle from him and gave it a neat twist, driving the metal screw deeper into the cork. Then she handed it back to him. "You'll force the cork into the bottle if you press too hard."

Garrick screwed the corkscrew all the way in, then pulled it out until it gave a slight pop. "How did you get into this business, anyway? It's not exactly a traditional career path, for a man or a woman."

"My family used to make wine. Did you bring glasses?"

"In the backpack." He watched as she leaned over and searched through the pack. "I take it your family's winery doesn't make wine anymore."

"Oh, it wasn't a winery. We just mucked it up in the barn and made enough to last through the year." She held up a pile of paper cups. "Is this all you brought?"

"It should be enough—"

"Glass or plastic would have been better. With these we won't be able to check clarity or see the legs."

His gaze fell automatically to her own long, sleek limbs. "The legs I'm seeing look just fine."

"You're looking in the wrong place," she said dryly, curling the limbs in question under her. She held out two of the cups. "Pour."

"So you used to make wine in a barn, eh?" He stopped pouring when the cups were halfway filled, as she directed. "It's a big step between 'mucking it up in a barn' and being a winemaker in Napa Valley."

She shrugged, lifted the cup to the sun, and tried to peer through the paper. "When I was a kid, it seemed like magic. All you had to do was press the grapes and leave them alone, and after a while you'd get wine." A ghost of a smile passed over her face. "My father used to tell us that wine fairies came down the Berkshires in the autumn, drank the grape juice, and spit up wine. I didn't believe him for a minute."

He watched her as she swirled the wine, thinking it was rather sad that as a little girl, Amanda didn't believe in magic.

"When I went to school, I was determined to find out how it all worked." She tilted the cup toward him. "So here I am, making a living out of sipping wine."

"Did you ever consider going back home and setting up a winery?"

"No. Western Massachusetts isn't the best grape-growing region in the world. Besides, we lost the farm a long time ago." She held her cup with two fingers, buried her nose inside, then lifted a brow in approval. "There's a certain procedure one follows when wine-tasting. Since we can't check color or clarity, we'll start with the bouquet . . ."

Garrick bit back his questions. The shutters had come down in those green eyes, and the coolness of her voice told him that she would answer no more. He had already learned more than he had expected. Amanda Karlson, winemaker extraordinaire, had once been a farm girl from western Massachusetts.

And she didn't believe in magic.

He listened politely as she explained how to swirl the liquid around the mouth, suction air through it, and then swallow. He watched with fascination as she took a sip and began making wonderfully erotic motions with her lips. He took a sip, more for sustenance than for art, thinking that the only correct way to taste wine would be to lick that last gleaming, ruby-colored drop off her lips.

She glanced around, then swallowed the wine. "You forgot one thing, Mr. Kane."

He winced as he swallowed. "What?"

"Something to spit out the wine into."

"God, I'm glad you said that." He grimaced into his cup and then looked at the bottom of the bottle.

"This one was in the 'obscene' price range, too. It tastes like chalk."

Amanda pressed the heel of her hand against her forehead. "Pearls before swine."

"Hey, you're the one who wanted to spit it out."

"You always spit it out when you're tasting. Otherwise, you'll be cross-eyed by the time you get to the last one."

"Oh. Kind of like a Berkshire fairy."

"I guess so." She smiled, a full-blown smile. "Come on, try again. This is a very solid Cabernet. It should taste herbaceous, with a little oak."

He took another sip, then grimaced. "Must be an acquired taste." He sat up, tossed the rest of the liquid in the grass, and looked pointedly at the bread and cheese. "Maybe I just need a good palate-cleaning."

"Seems to me you need a whole new palate."

She was teasing. Her eyes sparkled and her smile came easy and natural. He liked it. For the first time since he had known her, she looked relaxed. Inordinately pleased, he tore off two pieces of the sourdough, then pulled his Swiss Army knife out of his pocket and spread generous hunks of the sun-warmed Brie over the soft bread. He handed her a piece as she poked the cork back down into the neck of the Cabernet.

"So, Mr. Kane . . ." She laid the bread beside her and reached for another bottle of wine. "What do you do besides climb cliffs, make glow-in-the-dark pens, and buy wineries sight unseen?"

He bit into the tangy bread and looked at her, surprised that she chose to ask a personal question. Her attention was fixed on opening another bottle of wine. "I do a little of this, a little of that. Mostly just invest in different ventures."

"Sounds mysterious."

"What you do, in that laboratory with all those powders and beakers. *That's* mysterious. What I do is downright dull."

"If it's so dull, why have you kept it a secret from the entire Napa Valley?"

He stopped in midchew as she pulled the cork out of the neck of another bottle. She sent him a sidelong glance, and he thought that Amanda Karlson knew how to throw curve balls.

"Those people from *Winery* are coming tomorrow, so I assume the gag order on your identity is being lifted." She reached for two new paper cups. "It'll look strange if I know absolutely nothing about my own boss."

"There's nothing to know." He eased back down on his elbow, toying with the bread and cheese. "I was born and bred in New York City. Three sisters, two brothers—including Dominick."

"Big family."

"My mother is Italian and Catholic. My father had no choice—not that he minded."

She handed him an apple and a cup of golden wine. "Are they still in New York City?"

"They all live within twenty miles of the city. I bought this place in Dominick's memory, but I also bought it to get away from Manhattan." He placed the bread and Brie aside and shined the apple on his polo shirt. "I kept my identity secret simply because I wasn't in the mood to be inundated with invitations to Napa social events—yet."

She lifted her cup to the sun and tried to peer through the paper. "Kiss those days good-bye."

"So the PR firm warned me." He took a bite of the

crisp, tangy apple, and looked askance at the wine. "Is this stuff going to taste like tea and oak, too?"

She smirked. "You tell me."

Following her lead, he sipped it, swirled it in his mouth, bubbled air through it, and then swallowed.

"Well?" She looked at him expectantly. "What does it taste like to you? Butter? Ripe peaches?"

"Wine."

She laughed. A bright, spontaneous, unexpected sound. "You're hopeless, Garrick Kane, utterly hopeless."

"I can't be hopeless." He watched her. "I made you laugh, didn't I? That's the first time I've heard you laugh."

Her laughter died, but slowly. Her lips looked so soft, so moist, so full and ready to be kissed. He wanted to kiss her. Every muscle in his body strained forward, every nerve, every instinct, urged him to lean closer, to close the distance that separated them, to press his mouth against hers and taste the spice of the wine on her breath.

A breeze, cooled by the fog of the distant Pacific, passed between them, and rustled the oak leaves above them like soft music. The sun beat warm on the earth. The wine coursed through his veins and tingled in his blood. He waited for her to say something, to chill his ardor with a sharp comment or a cool tone of voice, but she said nothing. She kept looking at him. He saw that expression in her eyes again, that sleepy, languid, slightly dazed look that had sent him over the edge in the kitchen that day. She wanted him to kiss her. And God, he wanted so much to lean over, touch her soft skin, press her down beneath his body, and feel her open to him like a flower in the sunshine.

But if he kissed her now, she would never trust him again. For reasons he couldn't begin to analyze, right now Garrick valued her trust far, far more than he wanted a simple embrace on a late-August day.

He straightened, looked at his cup, then tossed the rest of the Chardonnay over his shoulder into the grass. "Well, Amanda, it's two down and four to go." He crushed the paper in his fist. "What do you say we get this over with so I can have a beer?"

FIVE

Garrick stood at the edge of the veranda, leaning on the trellis post, watching Amanda talk to the *Winery* reporter in the hot sun while the photographer stowed his equipment in preparation to leave. The small cassette recorder the short, stocky reporter had used throughout the morning now lay discarded on the dashboard of the sedan, a sure sign that the interview was over. Yet he lingered in the dusty driveway, a friendly smile on his face, asking just one more question.

She was working him like a marionette, Garrick mused, watching her nod and calmly explain some obscure aspect of winemaking. It was no wonder. She looked like a cool cherry Popsicle in her red suit, with her silvery-blond hair pulled back severely into a clip at the base of her neck. Those legs alone, exposed beneath a skirt that ended midthigh, were enough to drive a man to utter distraction.

But Garrick knew it was more than looks alone that

had turned the skeptical journalist who had arrived at his doorstep this morning into the fawning lapdog now pumping Amanda's hand with vigor. Garrick had been ready to throw the guy off a cliff after the reporter made a few snide comments about Amanda's youth and supposed inexperience. Amanda hadn't even blinked. As cool and untouchable as a queen in her own castle, she glided through the wine cellar, explaining her—rather, *their*—plans for the new Cedar Ridge Chardonnays. Within twenty minutes, the reporter ignored Garrick's existence and was earnestly asking Amanda's opinion on the future of a new variety of grape.

Garrick allowed his gaze to drink its fill as she waved farewell to the reporter and sauntered across the drive to her pickup. She retrieved a large bag from her truck, slipped the strap over her shoulder, and then walked toward the house. She had worn a touch of makeup today, and her lips looked luscious in muted red lipstick. He made a silent vow that someday he'd take her someplace where she would wear lipstick, and later he would kiss it all off.

"Well, they promised to come back for the Cedar Ridge opening," she said, glancing over her shoulder as the sedan disappeared down the unpaved road.

Garrick lifted his brows. Dominick used to take care of facing the media whenever they did anything unusual at Granite Investments, but Garrick knew enough about it to understand how important and how rare it was to secure free press coverage. He wondered if Amanda knew how much she was becoming less of an employee and more of a partner to him. "That's quite a coup, Amanda."

"I'll believe it when I see it," she murmured. "If

they really do give us two photo features in *Winery*, then we've made the big time.''

"He'll be here. Mr. Brodin won't miss another opportunity to speak to you."

"I didn't mean to monopolize the interview," she said, pulling off her sunglasses and glancing up at him, "but you weren't exactly the most talkative of owners."

Garrick shoved his hands into the pockets of his gray slacks. "After that incident in the wine cellar, I thought it best to keep my mouth shut."

"Well . . ." Those deliciously moist lips twitched in a smile. "They did look at you rather strangely after you insisted on calling the police."

"How was I to know a 'wine thief' was something you use to draw wine out of barrels?"

"I'm just glad I found it before they realized you really didn't know what I was looking for." She tucked her sunglasses in a pocket in the front of the shoulder bag. "Don't worry too much about it. They just think you're eccentric. Most winery owners are, anyway, and it makes good copy."

His gaze dipped to where the lapel of her suit crossed over, showing a V-shaped strip of her fair chest. "Did you know that Brodin was taking an interest in finding your tan lines?"

"Welcome to the world of sexism."

"You managed to turn him around."

"Not without a fight." She tugged a loose strand of hair back into the barrette at the nape of her neck. "Men are always amazed to find out that a woman can actually have a brain."

"Be fair, Amanda." He pushed away from the trellis. "In your case, it's hard for any red-blooded man to see beyond the packaging."

"Flatterer."

He grinned. Her comment had none of the coolness or the venom he expected. He even saw the corners of her lips twitch. Progress, he thought. Progress.

She nodded toward the door. "Would you mind if I changed inside? This 'packaging,' as you call it, isn't appropriate for working around the grape press."

"Sure." Garrick opened the door for her and followed her into the hallway. "I thought crush wasn't going to begin until tomorrow."

"No such luck. We tested the grapes on the western slopes yesterday afternoon and found they were ready for harvest." She headed farther down the hallway, toward the bathroom, while Garrick wandered down the three steps into the sunken living room. "With all this hot weather, we had to pick them today or risk the sugar content getting too high."

Garrick dropped into a white overstuffed couch which faced the large, brick-faced fireplace and crossed his feet on the glass coffee table. "I thought I saw Miguel pulling up a gondola full of grapes outside the cellar door."

"There's probably two of them by now."

He heard the bathroom door click shut. Immediately, his head filled with images of Amanda stripping off that sleek cranberry-red suit, standing on the plush blue rug in nothing but satin and lace undergarments. He closed his eyes and spread his hand over his face.

It wasn't ignorance that kept him silent through the *Winery* interview—not completely. It was getting harder and harder to hide his growing desire for the woman now shedding her clothes in his house. Garrick knew they would have a relationship beyond the boundaries of professionalism, despite Amanda's insistence to the contrary, despite his own restraint yesterday on the hill. Unlike Amanda, he refused to think of the unfinished chemistry experiment in his kitchen as a mere aberration. They would be lovers. As each day passed, as he grew friendlier with her, peeked a little more beneath the veil of her reserve, it was getting harder and harder to control his desire.

But faced with that sharp-eyed reporter today, Garrick had a new appreciation for Amanda's insistence that they keep their relationship professional in the eyes of the world. If Garrick had made a single move toward Amanda, one single slip that suggested they were more than just business associates, Brodin would have put Amanda on a spit like a roasting pig and let her burn in the fires of public opinion.

"It's going to be a long day," she said as she emerged from the bathroom in shorts and an old, grape-stained T-shirt, her suit slung over her shoulder. "I didn't have enough time to call all the cellar rats in, so we're working with a skeletal staff." She leaned against the low wooden railing near the stairs to the living room, peering at him in speculation. "You wouldn't have anything planned for the afternoon, would you?"

"Nothing but a cliff climb and a few phone calls."

Her gaze slipped over his body in a way that made Garrick's blood run hot. "I could sure put all those muscles of yours to better work in the winery than on that cliff."

"Amanda, honey, I know you could." He stood up, shoved his hands into the pockets of his gray suit, and sauntered over to where she stood. "What have you got in mind?"

"I need a volunteer." She shrugged, far too casually. "Just to help me around the cellar."

"Is that so?" Spend the afternoon in a dim room with Amanda? The possibilities were endless. "I'm all yours."

"You don't even know what you're getting into."

"I trust you."

"You're a businessman. You should know better than to sign a contract without reading the terms." Her eyes twinkled wickedly as she headed toward the door. "You just got yourself knee-deep in grapes."

Amanda burst through the back door of the main house and rushed headlong down the dim hallway. She knew the stairs to the upper floor were somewhere around here, on the left, and when she found them, she curled her fingers over the banister and took them two at a time. There was no time to waste—every second was precious—and she pushed open every door until finally, at the end of the second-floor hallway, she burst into Garrick's bedroom.

"Garrick!"

A faint bluish light spilled through the wide window that looked over the Cedar Ridge vineyards, casting a morning glow over the sleeping figure. Mindlessly, Amanda leapt onto the bed and shook one broad shoulder.

"Wake up, Garrick. Wake up!"

She glanced frantically around the room, still shaking him. Garrick grunted and rolled over. The sheet slipped down, showing a broad stretch of hairy chest and two well-sculpted pectoral muscles. He squinted up at her.

"I need an electric blanket." She scrambled off the side of the bed and threw open an armoire, only to find it full of suits. "You *must* have one somewhere around here. Where do you keep it?"

Garrick lifted himself on an elbow and rubbed his eyes. The sheet slipped down to his waist, exposing a taut washboard stomach and a narrow waist. He blinked at her blindly as she stood, arms akimbo, by his bed.

"Did you hear me? Tell me you have one. If I don't find an electric blanket soon—"

He reached for her, curling his hand around one of her wrists, tugging her with surprising strength back onto the bed. Off balance, she dug a knee into the mattress and clutched the warm skin of his shoulder.

"If you're cold, Amanda . . ." His hand slid around her waist and his voice was fuzzy with sleep, "you can just join me."

"Garrick, I'm *serious*."

"Mmm. So am I."

Amanda pressed against the width of his shoulders, but she was helpless as he wrapped his strong, muscular arms around her waist and lay back in the rumpled sheets, drawing her down with him. He wasn't wearing much beneath the linens, and with the fullness of her weight atop him, she felt every hard length of sinew, every distinctive contour of the man. She flattened her hands on the sheet on either side of his head and strained away, but that only brought their loins into more intimate contact.

He groaned sleepily, and ran his hands down her back to her buttocks as he lifted his head to kiss the hollow between her breasts. She felt the warmth of his lips through her T-shirt. She squeezed her eyes shut as her blood coursed in sudden heat through her veins, as every inch of her body tingled with awareness. His fingers found their way beneath the hem of her T-shirt and grazed the skin of her back. Amanda dug her fingers into the sheets as his hand found its way expertly to the strap of her bra and slipped under it, searching for a clasp. She sucked in her breath, for a moment forgetting herself, forgetting the crisis, forgetting everything but the feel of his bare, rough hand against her shoulder blade. His lips found their way to the neckline of her T-shirt, discovered the skin, and tasted it. Then she realized that his hand was working its way to the front, working its way to the fastening of her bra nestled between her breasts.

And she realized that this was no time for lovemaking—no matter how many times she had fantasized about it. She had an emergency on her hands.

"Garrick, stop." She rolled off him, clutching her chest for a minute to catch her breath. He groaned and reached for her again. She stood up and skittered away, backing up against the doors of the armoire.

He sat up, staring at her as if seeing her for the first time, peering at her in the dark. "Amanda?"

"Damn it, Garrick." She fumbled with the hem of her T-shirt, shoving it into the waistband of her cotton shorts. "You're not even awake, are you?"

"God, I hope I am." He shook his head sharply, as if to clear it of strange visions. "You're in my bedroom."

"I need an electric blanket." For the first time, she realized how provocative and ridiculous the request must sound. "I need it for the lab."

"This is one hell of a dream." He slipped his legs over the side of the bed. "Did you call me Garrick?"

"I'm going to call you something a lot worse if you don't help me."

He glanced at the clock on his night table, running a hand through his hair. "It's only six A.M."

"I know. I overslept." She tugged down on the edge

of her shorts, her anxiety returning in full force. "Every other migrant worker and winemaker in the valley has been up for hours, and I've been snoozing away while my fermentation tank practically freezes."

"Your what?"

"The fermentation tank. The one that had the faulty valve. I thought I fixed it, but this morning I took the temperature of the Chardonnay and realized it had broken again."

Garrick eased himself out of bed and walked toward her. Amanda's heart leapt to her throat. All he wore beneath that linen was a pair of white briefs, which did nothing to hide his state of arousal.

His very *impressive* state of arousal.

She flattened against the armoire, wondering how on earth she was going to resist this flesh-and-blood version of Adonis if he tried to kiss her. Suddenly, the fate of a batch of Chardonnay didn't mean much in the greater scheme of things.

"My robe."

She stared at him and released a noise—all she was capable of doing with Garrick standing only inches from her, aroused, warm, and rumpled from sleep, like the embodiment of all her recent, torrid fantasies.

"Amanda, I'm not fully awake yet." He placed his hand next to her head. His voice was a throaty growl. "If you don't let me get my robe out of that closet, I'm going to think this is still a dream, and then I'm going to drag you right back into that bed."

She pushed away, thanking God that the light was still too dim for him to see her flushing. She kept her back to him as he covered himself. Nervously, she ran her hand through her tangled hair.

He passed her and gestured to the door. "I think

there's an electric blanket in the linen closet. That *is* what you asked for, right?''

She nodded and followed him into the hallway, where he opened a closet and pulled a blanket off the top shelf. Once downstairs, Garrick slipped his feet into an old pair of sneakers, not bothering to tie the laces, and followed her sleepily through the back door of the main house. They crossed the driveway while the first pink fingers of dawn streaked the sky. The grape pickers already toiled among the vines, shuffling swiftly through the vineyard in the cool morning, filling plastic buckets full of grapes and dumping them in the gondola that waited at the end of the rows.

She pushed open the door to the cellar and focused her attention on the crisis before her. She rounded a pile of boxes full of bottled wine, then made a beeline to the broken tank. She bent among the tangle of wires and hoses to find an outlet for the blanket. Then she instructed a yawning Garrick to help her tape it around the stainless steel vat. Only when they had finished and she had put the blanket on low, did she breathe freely again.

She ran a hand through her hair, now completely free of the rubber band she had hastily wound around it when she awoke this morning, and observed their handiwork. ''That should do it. The temperature should go up in a little while.''

''It's cold as hell in here.''

''It's always about sixty degrees.'' She rubbed her arms, but she was too wound up to feel the cold. ''It's nice when it's hot outside.''

He sank down on a chair and stared at the covered fermentation tank. ''I've had women steal blankets before, but never quite like this.''

She glanced at him, unshaven and heavy-lidded, wearing nothing but a calf-length terry-cloth robe and a pair of battered sneakers. Now that the crisis had passed, she felt a little silly. The Chardonnay could have fermented just fine at the temperature of the cellar, but she always preferred to ferment the wine a little warmer, and since this was her first vintage at Cedar Ridge, she wanted everything to be perfect. "I'm sorry I dragged you out of bed so early."

He grinned, looking all the more charming for his dishevelment. "You did end a very interesting dream."

She flushed. She remembered that dream, and her body still tingled from the aftereffects. She had hoped he would have the grace not to mention it. She dug her fingers deeper into her arms and looked away from him.

"A little less sleep won't hurt me," he continued, stretching his legs out in front of him. "I suppose there will be a trailer full of grapes in front of this door before long, anyway, and you'll be standing over me, whip in hand, making me shovel them into that noisy press contraption."

"Complaining already?" She wandered over to a table full of hastily labeled beakers. She had already tested these samples of new wine, but last night, before she fell asleep, she hadn't had the energy to clear them away. She sat heavily on the end of a bench. "Crush has only just begun—most of the grapes haven't been harvested. And you did volunteer."

"Suckered by a pretty face." He rolled his shoulders beneath the robe. "You didn't tell me there were so many damned fruit flies around those gondolas."

"Welcome to the glamorous world of winemaking." She closed her eyes and rolled her head, trying to work the kinks out of her neck. "Wait until we harvest the cabernet. Your feet will be stained purple for a month just from standing in the gondolas."

"What's that cot doing here?"

Amanda didn't have to open her eyes to see the cot nestled against one side of the wall, and the tangle of knotted sheets. "I've been sleeping here. Someone has to keep an eye on the fermentation temperature, especially in this cranky tank."

"You could have slept in the house."

Unwittingly, his warm, soft bed came to mind—with him in it. She shivered, but not from the coolness of the cellar. "That would hardly be appropriate—"

"Appropriate be damned. You can't be getting a hell of a lot of sleep in this place." He sneered at the cot. "And that contraption looks more like the rack than a bed."

"It suffices."

"When was the last time you ate?"

"I'm fine." She rubbed the back of her neck, aching from one too many nights on the cot. "Crush is always like this. It'll pass and things will go back to normal."

"Yeah, in a month or two."

She heard his chair scrape. She looked up as he walked around and straddled the bench, just behind her. She stiffened as he swept her hair over one shoulder.

"Garrick, what—"

"Be quiet, Amanda. The crisis has passed. For five minutes, stop thinking about work."

Her response died in her throat as his hands, warm and strong, kneaded her neck, just in the spot where the crick had developed from sleeping at an awkward angle in the cot.

"Hell." He pressed harder at the base of her skull. "You're all knots."

She muttered something unintelligible. Her head fell forward and she closed her eyes, giving in for the moment to his touch. His fingers sought out and found every resistant muscle, every slight cramp, with expert swiftness, then kneaded and massaged until the tension passed. He worked his way down from the base of her skull, to her shoulders, digging his fingers deep into the lathes of muscle as stiff as boards, palpitating them until they softened. She moaned in utter pleasure as his thumbs worked their way down the length of her spine.

"Shh." His warm breath brushed her bare, exposed nape as she mumbled her appreciation. "Put yourself in my capable hands and relax."

She released a long, contented sigh. She hadn't realized how tired she was, how tense and anxious, until now, as she felt Garrick's hands working the stress out of her body. It felt so good just to sit and not think or worry or plan, it felt so good to have his hands on her back, to feel his fingers ease every strain, every tightness garnered over the past two weeks. His body radiated heat in the coolness of the cellar, a welcoming, comforting warmth. She felt like she was lying in a foamy, tepid bath while gentle waves lapped against her limbs. As he worked lower on her spine, his thighs brushed her hips. They surrounded her like a sort of shield, firm and strong. She felt safe here, calm and protected, strangely cherished under his touch.

Eons passed. At least it seemed like eons to Amanda. Her senses followed the brush of his hand greedily, anticipating each sweet feeling of release. When he pulled the hem of her T-shirt out of her shorts, she didn't protest. She told herself that this was just a friendly back rub, given by a boss who worried too much about her welfare. A fringe benefit of working for a playful, hedonistic man like Garrick Kane. Besides, the cotton of her T-shirt dulled his caresses, made them less effectual.

At least that's what she told herself.

He moved slowly, massaging his way back up from just beneath the hem of her shorts to the ribbonlike strip of her bra. His rough fingers scraped her skin, like the feel of fine sandpaper. Her flesh tingled. Slowly, other senses awakened under his caresses, heavy senses—the kind that pumped languorously through her blood, lazily, moving like dark molasses through her veins. He slipped his thumbs beneath her bra strap, ran them to either side, then back to the middle, then back out again. A little farther over her sides. A little closer to the curve of her peaked, suddenly aching breasts.

His warm lips touched the nape of her neck, right where the wispy tendrils of hair curled like baby's hair. Deep, deep in her consciousness, she knew she should pull away right now, but she was too drugged with relaxation to listen. It felt too good to stop—she was tired of stopping. She was tired of thinking. She wanted, just for this moment, to do nothing but feel.

She leaned back into him, closing her eyes, listening to his breath rush through his lips and warm her hair. She sank her head back against the curve of his shoulder. He kissed her temple, rasping his unshaven jaw against her forehead. His thumbs slid out of the wide strip of her bra, and then, within a breath, he gently cupped both her lace-covered breasts in his palms.

Her lips parted. She took a deep, shaky breath, her chest expanding into his hands. Her nipples hardened into tight, tingling knots. Sweet tension coiled in her lower abdomen. She arched her back, turning her head into his neck.

"Amanda . . ."

She hardly felt him unclasp her bra. All she felt was the sudden separation of the cups, the feel of the lace being peeled off her skin. Then his hands were there again, and the pads of his fingers scraped against the aching tips of her nipples.

She moaned. She heard herself, though she was hardly aware of making the sound. She turned her head toward him. Then his mouth was on hers, warm, insistent yet gentle, parting her lips. She opened herself to him, touched his tongue with her own, beckoned him to kiss her deeper. She grasped his knee beside her with one hand and wound her other around his head, drawing him down, closer, deeper, all the while her senses spun at the touch of his fingers on her breasts.

He made a noise, a sound ripped from somewhere deep in his chest. He stopped and stared down at her. She opened her eyes, twisting around and stretching her neck to find his lips.

"That wasn't all a dream this morning, was it, Amanda?"

She shook her head mindlessly, burying her hand deeper into his hair and urging him down. She groaned as he released her breasts and stood up. He drew her up and kicked the bench aside, sending it skittering a few feet on the concrete floor. He whirled her around to face him, forcing her to meet his dark-blue eyes for one moment before he wrapped her hard in his arms and kissed her.

No gentleness lingered in this kiss. He took what he wanted, and she gave, willingly. All the pent-up frustration of two weeks of wanting rushed to the fore. She clutched his biceps, as hard as granite beneath the terry-cloth robe, then dragged her hands up to wind them around his neck. His body was the only solid part of her world. The ground rolled beneath her feet, her senses whirled, and her body turned molten and molded against him. She closed her eyes as thoughts tried to intrude—not now, not now—while Garrick kissed her like a man possessed.

He tore away from her lips, bent and lifted her higher in his arms. He pressed her buttocks against the edge of the table. "Is there anything dangerous in these beakers?"

She blinked at him, now level with his face, not understanding his words.

"The beakers, Amanda," he said impatiently. "The ones on this table—"

"There's . . . there's nothing in them but wine."

Wine splattered all over the table, all over her back, as he cleared a space with one sweep of his hand. One beaker fell to the floor, crashing into pieces on the concrete. He pressed her down on the table, urging her thighs apart, his loins pressing flush against hers. From the deep, hazy recesses of her mind, Amanda heard a tiny scream of panic. Her eyes flew open. This shouldn't happen. This shouldn't be happening.

"Amanda? Is that you?" A high voice came from the doorway of the wine cellar. "Lordy be, I've never heard you break anything in my life."

She froze halfway down to the table, her thighs scraping against Garrick's hips. For a moment she stared into his eyes, too stunned to move, hoping beyond hope that she had just imagined the voice of Maggie Johnson in the cellar. Then she heard the door close and the sound of light footsteps.

Garrick reacted first. Clutching Amanda's hips, he put her feet firmly on the ground. Just as Maggie stepped into view from around the cases of wine, Garrick jerked his robe closed and took a single step back.

"Oh!" Maggie stopped in her tracks as she saw Garrick.

"Maggie! What a surprise." Amanda pushed away from the table. Amanda stared at her friend, who stared at Garrick, her hazel eyes widening. Amanda realized that Garrick was dressed in nothing but a pair of sneakers and a loose, almost-open terry-cloth robe—and Maggie knew it.

Maggie hugged a bundle close to her chest. "I didn't realize you had company, Amanda."

"Company? Oh, Garrick isn't *company*." Amanda tried to gather her senses. She crossed her arms and searched for something to say, searched for some way out of the awkward situation. Her gaze fell upon the electric blanket taped onto the fermentation tank. "I . . . I mean, *we*—Garrick and I—had to fix that fermentation tank this morning."

Maggie glanced at the mess on the table, the broken beaker, and the overturned bench. "It must have been one hell of a struggle."

"You were right about Amanda." Garrick's voice sounded deceptively calm in the tense atmosphere of the room. He tugged nonchalantly on the knot of his robe. "She's a workaholic. She has no qualms about dragging the boss out of bed at unearthly hours to get what she wants done." He shrugged. "No matter how clumsy he is."

One glance at Maggie's face told Amanda that her friend wasn't swallowing the bait. She could almost hear Maggie's gears churning.

"Yeah, well, Amanda has always been a little obsessive." Maggie held up a white bag with the name of a local bakery on it. "That's why I came. I thought you might need some coffee, Amanda, so I decided to stop in before going to work."

"Coffee."

"You know, that black stuff that runs in your veins?" She walked deeper into the cellar and placed the bag firmly on the table. "Looks like you could use a little professional help up here, too. Windsor won't notice if I arrive a little late."

Amanda still hadn't moved. Her tongue felt like a lead weight in her mouth. Maggie stood calmly, watching the two of them, showing no inclination to leave.

"I'll leave you two to work before I break any more beakers." Garrick looked at her pointedly. "When you're finished in here, Amanda, come up to the main house and let me know what we're going to do about that tank."

His eyes spoke a thousand words. He turned and walked through the cellar, the door closing behind him. Amanda sank against the table, not caring that rivulets of wine soaked into her shorts.

"Isn't it lucky I came?" Maggie asked. "A few more minutes and that fermentation would have completely overflowed."

Amanda looked up into her friend's piercing hazel eyes. "The situation was under control."

"Come on, Amanda. Your bra's unhooked. Don't tell me the fermentation tank did *that*."

There was no hiding the truth. With shaking hands, Amanda fumbled beneath her T-shirt and fixed her clothing. "You took the long way to Windsor, Maggie, if you stopped by here just to give me coffee. You could have had the grace to turn around and leave."

"Looks like I made it just in time. Do you want to tell me what's going on?"

"I don't know." She ran her hands through her hair. Now that Garrick had left the room and her hormones had gone from boiling to merely simmering, she began to realize what she had done. She had nearly slept with her boss, on a table in his wine cellar, without a single word of protest.

"This isn't like you, Amanda. Hell, he's the best thing I've seen for years, but I thought for sure you'd brush him off like you've done to a dozen others."

She closed her eyes and hugged her arms. She had let him touch her, she had let him lower her guard. For four days, they had worked so closely together. God, she was human, after all, and nothing could stop her from responding to the sight of him, bare-armed and handsome, standing knee-deep in the trailers, shoveling grapes into the press. But it had gone far beyond mere physical attraction. She had begun to see something wonderful in Garrick. He was an utter hedonist, but he wasn't afraid to get his hands dirty with grunt work. But more important, he respected her, as a winemaker and as a woman. He took orders from her without protest. He had asked her to be his teacher.

And he had made her laugh.

"Oh, Lord, how the mighty fall." Maggie placed the bag of coffee on the littered table and tugged a newspaper out from under her arm. "I came here to tell you to watch yourself, but it looks like I'm too late. Amanda darling, brace yourself. I don't think you're going to like what you're about to read."

She handed her the paper. Amanda took it in one hand, then unfolded it. It was the latest edition of the *Napa Weekly*, opened up to page 2.

Amanda's blood turned to ice.

In the middle of the page was a picture of Garrick in a tuxedo, with an exotic-looking brunette hanging on his arm. The headline read, ''Napa Ladies Beware! Notorious New York Playboy Buys Cedar Ridge.''

SIX

After so many years in Napa Valley, Amanda knew better than to listen to gossip, or to let an article like this get to her. The *Napa Weekly* was a notorious rag, yellow journalism at its most yellow. Yet as Maggie opened two cups of steaming coffee, Amanda absorbed every word of the article.

Twice.

He used to be a New York stockbroker. His company had engineered a dozen mergers, including one between the largest Japanese and one of the largest American airlines. He owned stock in too many corporations to count, and his net worth was rumored to be greater than the annual gross national product of certain South American countries. For years, his investment firm, Granite Investments, had been one of the bigger players in the wheeling-dealing, cutthroat world of Wall Street.

The article continued. He owned a collection of sports cars. It was rumored that he had paid over a hundred thousand dollars for a certain Joe DiMaggio baseball card. Two years ago, an influential New York magazine called him "New York City's Most Eligible Bachelor." His name had been linked with those of three world-famous models, two Hollywood starlets, and a sprinkling of European royalty. She reread the women's names several times, listed like so many trophies. The exotic brunette in the picture, the one who clung so intently to Garrick's arm, was the heiress to the Neptune comic book fortune.

She stared at his picture. It was Garrick all right, a little heavier but just as knock-down handsome in a well-cut tuxedo, his smile at full wattage. She wondered if the *Napa Weekly* had somehow mixed up the photo and the identity. The man they wrote about—the ruthless, determined businessman with a taste for women and fast cars—bore no resemblance to the man she knew as Garrick Kane. Could the same man who shoveled grapes for hours on end, spent his mornings rock-climbing, who dragged her away from her work simply to make her teach him how to taste wine—and then not kiss her—be such an amoral shark?

"One heck of a résumé, eh?"

Amanda glanced up at Maggie, who held out a cup of coffee. Amanda shifted the paper into one hand and curled her fingers around the steaming Styrofoam. "When did this come out?"

"Yesterday." Maggie righted the overturned bench and sat on it. "I tried calling you all last night but you weren't home."

She gestured vaguely to the rumpled cot. "I've been sleeping here."

"Have you?"

Amanda looked at her friend sharply. "*Someone* has to take the fermentation temperature readings."

"Amanda darling, don't be coy. You're talking to me, not Sadie Cello." Maggie tucked her legs beneath her and spread her tie-dyed skirt over her knees. "You and that berobed Hugh Hefner didn't look like you were taking temperatures or discussing stock prices when I walked in."

"It wasn't as bad as it looked." She tossed the paper on the bench beside Maggie and rubbed her forehead with the back of her hand. "I dragged him out of bed to find me an electric blanket for that . . ." She jerked her head toward the blanketed fermentation tank, "and things got a little out of control."

"I wonder if they said that before Vesuvius erupted." Maggie raised her hands in defense. "Sorry. Couldn't resist." She lifted up the paper and scanned the text. "You didn't know about any of this, did you?"

She thought about their lunch on the hill overlooking Sonoma Valley when she had glimpsed pieces of his past—a large family, a brother he obviously loved who had died young. She shook her head. "No. Not really."

All she knew about him was what she had seen and learned in the past two weeks. Handsome? She closed her eyes. She thought she'd get used to his looks, but he took her breath away each morning when she emerged from the wine cellar to see him perched on the side of the cliff, searching for a new route to the top. He acted more like a man on a leisurely vacation than a corporate warrior who had just invested in a winery. He even turned work into play. She still remembered the morning when he had dubbed her Snow White and the cellar rats the Seven Dwarfs, then insisted on singing "Whistle While We Work" while he shoveled grapes. She had been in tears with laughter all day, listening to the cellar rats' vain attempts to whistle on cue as they waddled around the cellar and the yard.

"You're in deep, aren't you, Amanda?"

Maggie gazed at her with compassion in her hazel eyes. Amanda felt a stab of terror. She couldn't be falling for Garrick Kane. No matter how handsome he was, no matter how funny, how kind. Amanda Karlson's cardinal rule had been *never, ever get involved with a business associate*. But it was more than that. The fear went far deeper. The last thing she wanted in her life was a messy entanglement; the last thing she needed was to lose control over her emotions, over her heart, over her *life*. Yet why else was she dwelling on the article in the paper, what else could explain the jealousy she felt when she thought of him in the arms of that exotic brunette? More importantly, why else did she give herself up so easily to the passion racing between them this morning?

Her fingers tightened over the coffee. Her emotions were so jumbled, so messy, and she strained to sort them out. She hated feeling like this—so uneven, so uneasy, so completely out of control of her own life. "This was just . . . hormones, Maggie." That was it, she thought, warming to the explanation. "I'm tired. I haven't gotten a good night's sleep in days." Stress can take many forms, she thought, and so can the release of tension. "We've been working a lot together lately, and you know how good-looking he is. Before I knew it, one thing led to another."

Maggie stood up and tossed her empty coffee cup in a nearby trash can. "Amanda, you can try to rationalize it all you want, but you've been standing in a puddle of wine since I got here."

Amanda looked down at her feet and saw the wet stains that spread over her canvas sneakers. She flushed, then stepped out of the puddle and took a long gulp of the coffee.

"Listen, I've been trying to fix you up with every eligible man in Napa since you came to Windsor, and nothing has ever lasted past the third date. I'd leap for joy if I found you splayed across a table with anyone else but Garrick Kane—"

"Maggie!"

"I'm not judging you. A woman would have to be dead not to react to that man." Maggie picked her oversize denim purse off the bench and slipped the strap over her shoulder. "But after reading that article . . . I just don't know. He's got too many notches in his bedpost, darling, and I don't want you to get hurt."

Amanda started as Maggie headed around the bench. "Where are you going?"

"I've got to get to Windsor. I'm late as it is." Maggie put her hand on her hip. "Leave with me. Take the afternoon off. Lie by the pool or go shopping or something. You could use a little time away from Casanova."

Amanda rubbed the lip of the cup against her chin. She couldn't leave. The chardonnay grapes were coming in faster and faster and it was time to rack the first batch of wine into aging vessels to make room for new fermentation.

"I didn't think so." Maggie clutched the strap of her purse with two hands. "Don't look so terrified. I won't leave you alone with the Big Bad Wolf. I suppose Windsor can do without me for a little while." She tossed the bag back onto the bench and glanced around the cellar. "Why don't we clean up all that broken glass before someone gets hurt, eh? I can fill you in on the latest scandal at Windsor.''

Maggie stayed, babbling about mutual friends and the upheaval at Windsor since Amanda had left, filling the wine cellar with distraction. Gratefully, Amanda turned to her work, checking the temperature of the fermenting Chardonnay, emptying out the beakers, and setting up the hoses for the first racking. The cellar rats, yawning, began to arrive for another day of work. As the light through the small cellar window lost its pink tinge and took on the gold glow of morning, Amanda began to breathe easier, losing herself in the endless, burdensome tasks of running a winery.

Maggie left with a hug as Miguel pulled the first gondola up to the press. Amanda watched her leave, then stood in the sunny yard, ordering a few cellar rats to shovel the grapes into the press. She kept her back to the main house, but the hairs on the nape of her neck prickled, and she knew she was being watched.

She would face him later, she told herself, returning to the coolness of the cellar. Right now, she was too unsettled. Besides, she had racking to do, to separate the clear wine from the lees. She walked to one of the fermentation tanks and checked the fitting of a hose, then drew the length of it through the rear door, into the caves, where empty oak barrels waited to be filled. Just as she finished clamping the hose onto the top of one of the barrels, the door creaked open.

His hands slipped around her waist, drew her back against the length and heat of his body. His warm lips searched beneath her hair for the bare, delicate skin.

''I thought Maggie would never leave—''

''Garrick, don't.'' She clutched his wrists and pushed them away. She turned and backed up against the oak barrel, resting her hand against one of the cold metal lathes.

"There's no one here." He pushed the door closed, as far as it could go, with a hose running through. "Come into the house with me. We'll tell the dwarfs it's a business meeting." He trapped her against the barrel, his voice as husky as the rustling of autumn leaves. "I've been thinking about you all morning . . ."

His words sounded so smooth, so practiced, as if he'd seduced a thousand women in the same way. She felt herself succumbing, even now. As he touched her face with his hands, she struggled away, slipped under his arm, pulled open the door, and stumbled into the main room. She pressed her hand against her lips, wondering if he had always sounded like that, but she had been too deafened by his charm to hear him properly.

"Amanda?"

She dropped her hand from her mouth and straightened her back. She turned and watched him walk into the room. "We've got to talk, Garrick."

"Talk?" An uncertain smile hovered around his mouth. "Hell, yes. We'll talk. There are just a few other, more urgent things I'd like to take care of first."

"I was tired this morning," she blurted, trying not to fall under the spell of those smoky eyes. "I've been stressed out for weeks. I haven't been thinking right—"

"The hell you haven't."

He reached for her. Startled, Amanda backed away. "Garrick—don't. It shouldn't have happened."

The smile died. He lifted his hands to his hips. "What's wrong?"

"Nothing's wrong."

"Liar." All levity left his face. "This morning you and I nearly made love—"

"Hush!"

"—right on that table." He pointed to the now-empty tabletop. "You weren't having second thoughts then, Amanda. What the hell did Maggie say to you?"

"Maggie has nothing to do with it." She swallowed dryly. "I've just come to my senses."

"Well, lose them again—I like you better without them."

She turned away, unable to face him or the fury of her own desire. He growled angrily, then paced around the room. His pacing stopped suddenly, and Amanda heard the crinkling of newspaper. She closed her eyes and flushed. She had forgotten that Maggie had left the *Napa Weekly* on the bench. Amanda felt as if she had been caught digging in his personal files. She hugged her arms and turned around, peering at his face as he read the article. His scowl grew darker and darker.

"Well, I figured the press vultures would find carrion sooner or later." He tossed the newspaper on the table with contempt. "They could have at least gotten a more up-to-date photo. That thing's nearly two years old." He pierced her with his gaze. "That's what Maggie came here to give you, isn't it?"

She couldn't deny it. She hugged her arms more tightly.

"Well, what the hell does it have to do with us?"

Us. As if there were something between them other than a professional relationship. She faced him, feeling the vibrant currents that always ran between them, no matter who was around or what the situation. She supposed they had a relationship, whether she liked it or not. They had shared intimacies that only lovers should share; they had almost shared the ultimate intimacy. The thought scared her to death. She was afraid of *us*, she was afraid of the need, she was afraid of what was happening between them.

"This has everything to do with 'us,' Mr. Kane—"

"Don't start on that 'Mr. Kane' crap, Amanda. We've gone too far for that." He gestured to the paper. "You can't possibly believe all that garbage."

"It's none of my business."

"I'm making it your business." He snatched up the paper and scanned the first few paragraphs. "Yes, I was a stockbroker. Yes, I lived in Manhattan. Yes, I dated beautiful women—"

"You don't have to explain yourself to me—"

"I didn't think I had to, but obviously I was wrong." He snapped the paper with a finger. "This is why I kept my identity a secret for so long. I knew some rag would make me sound like a lascivious corporate king. Hell, maybe I was at one time. But things have changed. You're a scientist. You should believe the evidence of your own two eyes."

"It doesn't really matter." She could handle his anger. Anger was something she understood, something she could manage. She dropped her arms and squared her shoulders. "That article only makes it all the more important that I keep a professional distance from you."

"Ah, then we're back to the gossip again."

"You've been branded a playboy, Mr.— Garrick." She glared at him. "I don't want to be branded as just another one of your playthings, just another conquest."

"So you're just going to put all this back in a bottle somewhere and stopper it."

"It should never have come out of the bottle in the first place."

"Too late." He walked to her side, almost daring her to run away. "Something special happened here this morning, Amanda, something that had been developing since we first met. Don't tell me you didn't think so, too."

She looked away from his dark-blue eyes, fixed her gaze on his T-shirt, stretched far too tight across his chest. Something had been growing between them, something strong and powerful and utterly undeniable. Something she couldn't control. Something she was afraid of bringing into her life.

"You're afraid of more than just gossip, aren't you?"

His voice was deep, ragged, and she felt his breath on her hair. She couldn't look up. Her insides had begun to melt, like wax before the heat of a blazing fire.

"You're afraid of a little magic. You're scared to death of taking your hands off the wheel, even for a minute."

How could he know? How could he know all the fear she hid from the world?

He gripped her shoulders. She flattened her hands against his chest. A muscle flexed in his cheek. "Life doesn't always work the way you plan it, Amanda. It doesn't follow rules. It's full of earthquakes and hurricanes and, every once in a while, unexpected passion in unexpected places." He lowered his head so that his lips were only a few inches from hers. "Every now and again, you've got to take a risk, otherwise life isn't worth a damn."

Her lids fluttered closed over her eyes, and she

waited, waited, for the feel of his lips on hers. She ached for them, she wanted them, despite all her words to the contrary. Moments passed. She blinked her eyes open. He stared at her, his desire bald and naked in his eyes, waiting for her to make the first move. Waiting for her to *choose* to take the risk.

And she knew she couldn't. Not willingly, not with all her senses about her. The stakes were far too high. He had no idea what he was asking of her. He had no idea how long she had lived in insecurity after her father died, scraping pennies together with her mother to feed and clothe her and her two sisters, wondering if they'd make the next rent payment, working two jobs through college and sending money home, all to get to where she was today. He was rich. He could do anything. She had one anchor in her life, one source of constancy, of security, one thing that would never die on her—her career. Having a torrid affair with her own playboy of a boss was one thing that could definitely set it back.

But there was more than this. There was fear—stark, dark terror—flowing through her veins. How many years had her mother lived in darkness after Dad died? Amanda would never forget the flat emptiness in her mother's eyes, the long nights of muffled crying, the endless, aching despair, the utter desolation, the loneliness she could never hide no matter how hard she tried. *That* was the reward for fifteen years of love—for fifteen years of dependence. A long time ago, Amanda swore she would never love like that, she would never risk all that pain. Why, why now, after all these years of turning men away, of drowning in her work, was Garrick Kane knocking at the door of her heart?

Her hands shook as she pushed him away. "Garrick, I don't want this . . . in my life."

He cursed, loudly, then stepped away. He strode to the paper, crushed it in his hands, and tossed it in the garbage. He ran his hands through his hair in frustration. "Someday, Amanda, you'll realize there's more to life than what you find among these burners and bottles." Then he glared at the electric blanket strapped around the fermenter. "I hope that will keep you warm at night."

After Garrick left, Amanda stood for a long time, alone, in the cool, damp air of the cellar, shaking uncontrollably, feeling like her heart had just been torn out by the roots.

Garrick flexed his hand over the phone as his mother launched into an involved tale about the recent shenanigans of his younger brother, Luke. Wearily, he leaned back in his chair and propped his sneakered feet on his desk. The bare skin of his back stuck against the leather, for he hadn't yet changed out of his climbing gear before coming to the study to work. He reached down and picked up a bottle of spring water on the floor, lifted it to his lips, and drank deeply, clearing his mouth of dust.

Someone knocked at the door. His body tensed. He knew it was Amanda—he had been waiting for her.

He dropped the bottle back to the floor. "It's open."

Amanda walked in and hesitated. He waved her in, gesturing to a seat.

"It's nothing, Ma—someone just came in." Garrick watched Amanda as she ignored the chair and began wandering, arms crossed, around the room. "So what's the ending to all this? Is Luke still in that South American jail or has he made it home?''

His mother continued the tale. Garrick switched ears and watched Amanda, who seemed to have found an old painting on the wall of extraordinary interest. An oversize U. C. Davis sweatshirt drooped off her shoulders, and she wore faded jeans—a sure sign that she'd spent the bulk of the day inside the cool wine cellar and not in the bright September sun. Of course, one look at her pale face told him the same thing. The woman looked like she hadn't seen the light of day for years—or at least for the past ten days, since that sizzling morning in the wine cellar.

She turned and glanced at him over her shoulder. She looked pointedly at her watch, and mouthed the words, 'I'll come back later.'

"No. Stay." He dropped his feet off the desk and leaned forward. "Ma, there's someone here and I've got to go. But listen—I'm glad Luke's home, but you've got to keep him there until next month." He paused as his mother complained. "I don't know how. Try feeding him your lasagna every night. Just don't let him go bolting off to another Third World country, will you? I want him here with the rest of the family for the winery opening." Garrick looked up at Amanda and shrugged. "All right, Ma. Talk to you soon."

Garrick slapped down the antenna of the portable phone and tossed it on the desk. He hazarded a smile. "My mother could probably win some international competition on long-windedness."

She smiled tightly. He noticed the faint purple smudges beneath her eyes, the corded tendons of her neck. She obviously hadn't had a good night's sleep in weeks. She had lost weight, too. He could see it in the sharp jut of her clavicle, the deep hollow of her shoulder. She stood like a frightened deer, only a few feet into the room, looking like she'd bolt at the first sign of danger.

Cool Amanda Karlson wasn't as invulnerable as she thought, Garrick mused. About the only part of her body that wasn't tensed up like a taut wire was her mouth. Her lips looked soft, vulnerable, as if the faintest touch would bruise them.

Something squeezed around his heart.

"You wanted to speak to me, Garrick?"

She gazed at him evenly, waiting, all business, as usual. For the past ten days the only conversations they had were terse and abrupt—mostly updates of how crush was going or what purchases she had to make to keep the winery running. Business over, they went their separate ways. Well, business was about to throw them together, and often.

He reached for a pile of mail on one side of his desk. "Since that damn article came out in the *Napa Weekly*, I've gotten a lot of invitations—to brunches, new wine tastings, soirees." He flipped through the envelopes like a deck of cards. "According to the PR firm, I have to accept every one of these invites if I want anyone to come to the Cedar Ridge opening." He looked Amanda straight in the eye. "According to the PR people, you have to come, too."

She started. Visibly. Terror flickered through those clear green eyes. Inwardly, he cursed. He had expected such a reaction, but it yanked at his heart to see her so afraid. Whatever fears hid beneath Amanda's cool exterior ran deep—maybe too deep for him to unearth, too deep for him to soothe. Still, how had he messed things up so badly? He had been patient. He had made her laugh. He had waited until she opened herself up to him. And she *had* been ready for him—fiery and passionate, kissing him with abandon, falling back on that table, her neck arched, her lips soft and willing . . .

He forced the memory out of his head. He couldn't think of that—not now, not when he had to convince Amanda to come with him to all these parties.

"Amanda, this is business." He tried to sound direct and firm and sensible, when all he wanted to do was take her tense body in his arms and make love to her until she softened and surrendered to him, and to whatever demons she battled inside. "I own the place, and you're the creative mind behind it. We have to go together, as the owner and winemaker of Cedar Ridge."

"Of course we do." She swallowed, and the tendons stiffened on her neck. "The winemaster at Windsor used to go to these things all the time. It's the best way to get the Cedar Ridge name known around the valley." She rubbed her arms. "With crush on and all, I had forgotten all about it."

He glanced at the bones standing out in the back of her hands, the way her nails dug into her sweatshirt. "Are you sure you can handle it?"

Her eyes flashed. "What is that supposed to mean?"

"I mean, with all the work in the cellar—"

"I'll delegate some to the cellar rats." She tilted her chin in challenge. "Do you have any complaints about my work product?"

"None at all." *Except there might be too much of it.* "I just want you to be prepared."

"For what?"

"For talk." He watched as her eyes narrowed. "We'll be going to these parties together. A 'Notorious Playboy Stockbroker' and an unattached woman." *A beautiful, fragile, frightened woman.* "The *Napa Weekly* will have a field day—"

"There will be no rumors," she insisted, "as long as you behave yourself."

Behave myself. As if he were a five-year-old boy with his hand in the cookie jar. He wondered if she had any idea what kind of self-control he'd used since he met her—if she had any idea the depths of his wanting. Hell, he wanted to see her name linked with his, if for no other reason than to keep all other men at bay, but he'd sacrifice that comfort for the sake of her trust. He wouldn't make a move toward her in a public place. And he'd beat the stuffing out of any man who suggested she was nothing but his plaything. Amanda Karlson was too important to him. How important, he was just beginning to realize.

"You should know by now that you can trust me, Amanda."

She didn't respond. Her lashes swept down over her cheeks. The fax machine on his desk coughed into life and began spitting out another transmission, the fourth that day.

He ignored it and pushed the pile of invitations toward her. "Here. Take a look at these. The first one is a luncheon at the Vintner's club tomorrow."

"Tomorrow?!"

"I probably should have told you sooner, huh?"

She reached for the pile and began sorting through the invitations. She sucked her lower lip between her teeth. "There must be two or three of these things a week."

Two or three chances a week to prove to you that I can be trusted, that gossip can be avoided, that there is something between us, Amanda, that rarely happens

between a man and a woman—and that it's worth the
risk to discover it.

She leaned a hip on the chair across his desk. He
watched the tendons in her neck flex, watched the
quick, sharp movement of her fingers as she shuffled
through the invites. He could see the tension growing
in her body. He hated watching her twist into knots.
Though Amanda was quieter in her stress, she reminded
Garrick of Dominick just before a big deal—pacing,
barking orders, smoking a cigarette, pulling on his hair,
the veins in his forehead throbbing. Later, after Dominick had died, Garrick always wished he had dragged
his brother to the health club for a game of racquetball
when he was that highly strung. Amanda would spit
nails if he offered her that kind of invitation, especially
after all that had happened between them.

Then he thought of an idea.

"Look at this!" She lifted out one invitation written
in swirling gold leaf. "We've been invited to the
Georges Duchamp affair. This is the poshest event of
the season."

"Amanda—how good are you at table hockey?"

She looked up at him with that stunned-rabbit look
in her eyes. "What does table hockey have to do with
the Georges Duchamp ball?"

"Nothing. I just bought the game and I need your
help." He stood up and rounded the desk, determined
to get her into the game room before she fully came to
her senses. "Come downstairs. I've been wanting to
try it out."

He walked out of the room with authority, pleased
when he heard her hesitant footsteps behind him. He
passed the kitchen and opened the door to the cellar,
flicking on the light switch. He galloped down the stairs

and padded across the wall-to-wall carpeting where the game stood in the middle of the room.

Amanda followed more slowly, pausing at the base of the stairs, still gripping the stack of invitations in her hand. "Garrick—"

"It's all ready to go." He stood on one side, ostentatiously pulling the levers until the players were correctly lined up for the beginning of a game. "I'll be blue. You'll be red." *It's a great color on you.* "Tell me if you think that goalie is sticking."

Speaking in the imperative always worked magic on people who were unsure or hesitant about a situation. He had closed a hundred deals that way. The technique worked perfectly on Amanda. She floated across the room, still stunned, like she couldn't quite believe what she was hearing or what she was doing.

She put the invitations on a nearby chair and took a position at the other end of the waist-high miniature hockey rink. "I don't know how to play."

"It's simple." Garrick dropped a small black puck in the middle of the board. "Move your men by pulling the levers. The idea is to get that black puck into my net and to stop me from doing the same to you."

He set the timer. Amanda jumped as it buzzed loudly and the game began. He got control of the puck and immediately knocked it down to her side. Startled, she fiddled with the levers, trying desperately to move the puck out of her zone, making a triumphant little noise when she managed to flick it down the boards to his side of the rink. Undaunted, he returned it, determined to keep her on guard.

Eventually, he scored the first goal. She straightened and frowned as he knocked the timer. "Looks like you won. I really should—"

"It's not over yet. There's ten minutes left in the first period," he explained. He set up his men and placed the puck back into the center. "Come on, you're not so bad at it."

She leaned over the board. He knocked the timer, springing into action as the buzzer rang.

They played out the first period. Before she could find an excuse to leave, he told her there were two more periods in the game. She narrowed her eyes, but leaned over the game and played, more aggressively than before. Soon enough, all her attention was focused on the little black puck, and she periodically cursed the goalie, who, she insisted, stuck at all the wrong times. He smiled, and urged her attention back to the next face-off.

By the time the game ended, Amanda was bouncing around her end of the rink, intent on making that last goal to even up the game. But he swept a man around hers and struck—and then the buzzer went off to signal the end of the last period.

Garrick grinned as he straightened victoriously. She was breathing a little fast, and some color stained her cheeks. She flashed him a set of reproachful green eyes. "No fair," she said. "You've played before."

"Oh, maybe a few times."

"A *few* times?" She shoved the levers deep into the rink. "You probably spend nights doing this with Miguel. Besides, my goalie sticks."

"Change sides and we'll play again."

She agreed wordlessly. She pulled resolutely on the bottom of her oversize sweatshirt and headed around the table. As she clutched the levers, poised on her side, she straightened and leaned a hip against the game.

"Come on, Amanda." He noticed that she was looking at him strangely, suspiciously. "We'll play best of three."

"Actually, I'll pass on the next game." She pushed away from the table. "It's time I got back to work."

"Don't be a sore loser—"

"Old trick, Kane, but I'm not falling for it." Something flickered in her eyes. "I've got a tank of Chardonnay to rack."

He followed her as she headed across the room, toward the stairs. He could see the tension returning in the stiffness of her neck and shoulders. She rounded the banister and took the first step, but he stopped her by placing his hand on the banister, just above hers. "You've been working too hard."

"It's crush." She shrugged. "Everyone's working hard."

"On you, it shows."

Her eyes narrowed, then she started to head up the stairs, determined to ignore him.

He grasped her wrist, stopping her. "Just one more game—"

"I said no."

"I said *yes*." His voice hardened. "I'm making it an order. Call it business recreation. Enforced R&R."

"I'm your *employee*, Mr. Kane, not your playmate." She yanked at her wrist in vain. "I'm here to make wine for Cedar Ridge, not to fulfill your whims. I don't have time for this—"

"You don't have time for anything these days, do you? Not for sleeping or eating, and definitely no time for blowing off a little steam." He scanned her body thoroughly, his anger growing. "You're turning into a bag of bones."

"If you kept your eyes to yourself you wouldn't notice."

"That's a physical impossibility. You're too damned good-looking, Amanda, even when you're half dead with exhaustion—and I'm not going to let you kill yourself in my winery."

"You overestimate your influence on me—"

"Hell, I wish it *was* me. I wish you were working yourself blind because you can't get that morning in the wine cellar out of your head. Hell, I can't. But I know that's not the reason you spend every day here. You'd work yourself to death all on your own."

All his rage rose to the surface. He hadn't told Amanda or anyone else why he had left Manhattan for the hills of this winery. He hadn't thought it would ever be necessary, yet even here, among the rustling vineyards, he found himself watching history repeat itself.

Except this time, he could do something about it—but only if Amanda let him.

"I've seen this before, Amanda." He stepped up on the edge of the stair, level with her face, with nothing between them but the lathe of the redwood banister. "I knew a man who worked like a demon, day and night, so obsessed with his job that he went through two wives in the course of seven years. One day I came into the office to find him slumped over his desk. I thought he was sleeping, until I touched his shoulder." Garrick still remembered the feel of that shoulder beneath his hands—cold and clammy and lifeless as a hunk of stone. "He was dead, Amanda. Dead of a heart attack at the age of thirty-six."

She stopped struggling. She stared at him with wide green eyes.

"I should have seen it coming. All those fancy dinners, all that smoking, all those high-stress, reckless business deals. I didn't notice, though, because I was living the same lifestyle." Unconsciously, Garrick tightened his grip on Amanda's wrist. "He was my brother, Amanda. He was only two years older than me." He glared at her, forcing her to face the truth. "Dominick worked himself to death. And now I'm watching it happen to you."

SEVEN

Amanda stared into Garrick's dark blue eyes. His raw anguish lay exposed to her gaze like the bleached bones of an old shipwreck—a reminder of a tragedy long past but not forgotten.

Her heart turned over in her chest. She understood this agony. She knew how it felt to take for granted the comfort of someone's presence, and then abruptly be faced with a lifetime without it. She understood the endless heartache, the sense of despair, the anger against the powers that be who sought fit to steal a life away—especially when that life was in its fullest flower.

She understood something else, too. Ten days ago, she had read in the *Napa Weekly* about a playboy, a shark in the business world, and she had doubted Garrick's sincerity and her own sanity because the man she read about was not the man she had come to know. Now she realized that the old Garrick was dead. He died with Dominick. The man standing before her was a man transformed in the wake of his brother's demise.

The realization brought her no comfort. It only frightened her more. This man had the power to affect her in ways no other man ever could. She had spent the past ten days hiding from herself—drowning herself in her work in a vain attempt to forget what had happened between them in the wine cellar that unforgettable morning. Now she realized that she had only been hurting him by dredging up raw memories of his brother's untimely death. And now she felt guilty and cruel, for fighting with him about a simple table hockey game, for forcing him to expose this sore part of his soul to her gaze.

She squeezed his hand. She wanted to say something to show how much she understood, but she knew words were utterly inadequate. What she really wanted to do was round the stairs and wrap her arms around him . . . but she knew that once in his embrace, she wouldn't be able to stop herself from giving him all the comfort a woman could give a man. And so she stood silently, gazing into his eyes, fighting the irresistible urge to enfold him in her arms, to bury her own face in his strong shoulder, to lose herself to his unbearably potent pull—all while her heart lay open and aching for him.

Finally, he released her hand, then stepped off the stair. He rubbed the back of his neck and avoided her eyes. "I didn't mean to unload all that—"

"No—I'm glad you told me." She smiled at him, softly, hesitantly, still not trusting herself, unsure of this strange situation, unsure of how she could comfort him without exposing her own weakness. "I know how you feel, Garrick. I lost someone once. Someone I loved. Very much."

Suddenly, he was alert. Expectant. Waiting. Color crept to her cheeks. She knew she would have to tell him now; she could not expect him to let a statement like that pass without comment. She looked away and absently pecked with her fingers at an old piece of tape on the railing.

"When someone dies," she began, "I know how the pain, and the memories, can sneak up on you." She struggled to find a way to express a feeling for which there were no words. "It's like . . . it's like someone has rearranged a favorite room in the night without telling you. Long after it's done, you keep bumping into things."

He was silent for a moment, then he asked, "Are you still bumping into things?"

She nodded. "For years, I still expected to see him in the doorway when I got home. Even now, I think of things to tell him, find things I'd like to show him, see gifts in stores that I think he'd like." She tried to swallow the lump forming in her throat, failed, and instead forced a strained laugh through it. "He would have liked you. He was very . . . playful."

Garrick made an uninterpretable grunt. "I suppose it's good to know that your former lover would have approved of me."

She started, realized Garrick's error, then gave him the shadow of a smile. "He wasn't a lover, Garrick. He was my father."

He squeezed his eyes shut. When he opened them again, he reached for her. "Christ, Amanda, I'm—"

"I know." She drew her hand away from the intimacy. She had told him too much; she felt exposed. Vulnerable. All this talk of Dad had brought back the memory of those years: the empty, quiet farmhouse;

Mom's tears—and the sobbing she could never muffle in her pillow—and the dead look in her eyes. It was a sort of hell, to be that vulnerable. Amanda never wanted to be that vulnerable.

She drew herself up. She was being selfish. She was dwelling on her own pain; Garrick's loss was still raw while hers had long developed a hard and protective scar. "I'm glad you told me, Garrick."

"I'm glad you told me, too." He jerked his head at the table hockey game. "What do you say we drown our mutual sorrows in a game of table hockey?"

She dug her fingers into her sweatshirt and balled it into her palms. To be alone in a room with him was a dangerous thing, even more dangerous when she felt these ties growing between them, the kind of ties that only grew between good friends . . . or lovers. But he was asking her to play for her sake alone, and to deny him was to be even more selfish, to exalt her own fears above his pain.

"Amanda . . . don't say no." Their gazes met and locked. "You're special to me—as an employee, as a woman, as a friend. Hell, you know that by now. Don't make me watch you destroy yourself."

She wondered if he knew how deeply his words penetrated, if he knew how much she had yearned to hear those words—and feared them just as intensely. Garrick burrowed his way deeper and deeper into her heart with each passing day. She didn't want to care about someone this much. She didn't want to need someone like Garrick.

She never wanted to need anyone.

"Come on . . ." His voice turned cajoling; his eyes showed the first sign of sparkle. "I'll even promise to behave."

He was teasing her, determined to disperse the dense atmosphere that had built up between them. She tilted her head, as if she were seriously contemplating the issue, though she knew in her heart what she must do. "I don't know. It's not an equal match-up."

"I'll spot you a one-goal advantage." He stepped back, toward the table, his pain hidden again under the gleaming tide of his playfulness. "I'll even let you play the blue side, where the goalie doesn't stick."

She watched him as he strode to the table and stood, poised and ready on his side. He tugged in impatience on the levers.

Friends, she thought as she slid her hand along the banister and rounded the stairs. There was nothing wrong with just being friends.

Amanda pipetted precisely three milliliters of solution into a flask. For the first time all day, the cellar was silent; the cellar rats had left for the evening and the endless basketball game had ended, along with the incessant banging on the side of the building where Garrick had nailed up the basketball hoop. She had been looking forward to the quiet all day. Now, surrounded by silence and by the faint, tangy aroma of fermenting grapes, she could finally get some analytical work done in peace.

Suddenly, the door burst open and the late-afternoon sun streamed into the cool room. Garrick's voice carried from one end of the cellar to the other. "All right, Karlson. Time to get out on the field."

She groaned, then placed the flask at the end of a long row of similar flasks and glared at Garrick through her safety glasses as he strode into the room. "I've already had my daily intake of play today." She deliberately picked up another empty flask and added three milliliters of solution to it. "I came in fourth at this afternoon's table hockey tournament and I even played one game of "Out" with the rats."

"This is different." He grinned and tugged on the creased bill of his Yankee baseball cap. "This is business."

She lifted a skeptical brow. He was wearing shorts and an old sweatshirt cut off at the sleeves and waist, exposing the bulging muscles of his arms. A dark-gray V of sweat stained the front. She forcefully dragged her gaze away from the strip of lightly furred abdomen exposed beneath the edge of his cut-off sweatshirt. "You always did have a strange sense of what was appropriate business attire."

"This is appropriate. Put those things down and take off that lab coat. We've got to practice."

"Practice what? Your new video game?" She shook her head and reached for another flask. "Sorry, Kane, but these sulfur dioxide measurements are a lot more important than Baby Godzilla in Mushroom Land."

"Yeah, but they're not as important as the Spring Winery League Charity Baseball Game."

"Oh, God." She squeezed the black rubber bulb, sucked up three milliliters of solution into the pipette, then poised the tube over another empty flask. "That thing isn't until next May. Have we been invited to it already?"

"We're playing in it." He circled the ball in the palm of his mitt. "You're in left field."

The pipette slipped through her fingers, fell into the flask, and clattered around the glass neck.

Garrick grinned. "Should I have safety glasses on or something?"

"Left field?!"

"Hey, I tried to get you on first base, but I talked to the cellar rats today, and frankly, Amanda, they doubted your ability."

"You decided this last night, didn't you? At the wine tasting?"

He shrugged. "Some of the other owners invited Cedar Ridge to take part in the event. How could I refuse?"

She frowned. She had wondered why Garrick and a few other owners had slipped off into a corner last night, during one of the more important social events of the season. She thought Garrick had been doing it just so he wouldn't have to take part in the tasting. Now she realized he had been pressing the flesh as diligently as she had, trying to weasel in on the upper crust of the winemaking society. "You should have asked me, Kane." She pushed the flask aside. "I've never played softball in my life."

"Which is why we have to practice."

"Oh, no." She shook her head. "I'm not making a fool out of myself in front of the entire valley. You're getting me off the team."

"Out of the question. You know how much publicity this game gets every year. A new winery and all, we need as much free publicity we can get. Plus, it's a big charity event. Raising money for the kids in that hospital in Yountville."

She glared at him. It was true, the annual baseball game was the major fund-raiser for the Yountville Hospital's children's wing, and every winery of note took part. Also, every paper in the region covered the games. The Windsor Winery was big enough so she never got forced into playing for their team, but Cedar

Ridge had barely enough players, even if they included the cellar rats they had hired on a temporary basis.

"You're a sneaky rat, Garrick Kane." She placed another flask in front of her, firmly, hoping beyond hope that he'd back off. "But the game isn't until next spring."

"Something tells me you're going to need eight months of practice."

She frowned at him. "These sulfur dioxides have to be done a heck of a lot sooner."

"They can wait until after dark. Softball can't." He glanced out the single window of the cellar. "We've only got about an hour of daylight left."

She sighed and pulled off her latex gloves finger by finger, knowing that it was useless to fight. For two weeks, since the first table hockey game, Garrick had burst into the wine cellar at all hours, demanding she play one game or another. Every time she protested he gave her a look, as if she were working herself to death just by refusing. She always succumbed. Guilt, she mused, unbuttoning her lab coat as she followed her whistling boss, was a powerful motivator.

Outside the cellar, the air was still balmy from the warm September day, but the first feathery fingers of fog curled over the eastern ridge, accompanied by a tangy Pacific breeze. She tossed her lab coat over the edge of the press. The sound of cornets and Spanish guitars drifted up from the trailers and cars of the migrant workers parked on the other side of the winery.

He picked up a bat which lay in the middle of the driveway. He dusted it off and held it out to her, skinny end first. She took it, then glanced around the yard. "Aren't the rats being forced into practice, too?"

"They were too beat from basketball to hang around.

I'll get them tomorrow.'' He took her elbow and drew her into a box whose outline he had dug into the dirt. His voice dropped a husky octave. "Besides, I thought you'd want a little private tutoring.''

She slung the bat over her shoulder, glaring at him suspiciously, thinking that she had gone out of her way to avoid private *anything* with Garrick.

He drew her deeper into the box, ignoring her look. "Are you a righty or a leftie?''

"I'm right-handed.''

"Here. Stand like this.'' He whirled her around and stood behind her. He tossed his mitt and ball into the dust.

Suddenly, she felt his warmth, from the back of her head to the back of her knees. He leaned over her. His arms came around her. She started.

"Easy, Amanda.'' He backed away a little and lifted up the bat, still tight in her grip, with one hand. "I'm just going to show you how to hold this thing.''

She flushed, feeling foolish for reacting so strongly. He hadn't touched her since that morning in the wine cellar. Just because she had fantasized about him every day and every night, just because her heart thumped harder at the feel of his arms around her, there was no reason to believe he felt the same explosive passion. They were friends now. Just friends.

She gripped the bat with both hands and forced her voice to remain even. "Isn't this how it's held?''

"Not quite.''

His bare, brawny arms came around her again. Engulfed in his warmth, she closed her eyes as he adjusted her grip with the lightest touch of his rough, calloused hands. She felt the heat and dampness of his sweatshirt against her shoulder blades. She felt his cheek against her hair.

"Bring it up over your shoulder. Like that." He brushed her inner wrist as he guided the bat over her right shoulder. "Spread your stance a little—" He nudged her ankles with one foot until her feet were spread to his satisfaction, oblivious to the way the gesture made his loins press intimately against her buttocks. "Now lean forward and bend your knees."

Leaning forward, she discovered, only made her hips thrust more deeply against his.

"Good." He pointed toward a small, packed mound of dirt. "I'm going to be standing there. I'm going to throw the ball, and you have to keep your eye on it. Watch it until it's over the plate. Then you'll swing. Like this."

His hands covered hers again. Slowly, he brought her through the motions of swinging the bat. Her back lay full against him as he extended her arms. He spoke quietly against her hair, his breath warming her skin. She smelled the spicy, male scent of him, the heady odor of dust and sweat and sun-warmed skin. She didn't hear a word he said.

"Understand?"

She nodded mutely, hoping he'd back away and leave her alone with her rushing blood. She tried in vain to dry her sweaty palms on the ashwood of the baseball bat.

"Okay, let's see what you're made of, Karlson."

He backed away, retrieved his mitt and baseball from the ground, then jogged to what he had marked as the pitcher's mound. Amanda took a long, deep breath to try to calm her elevated pulse. *Concentrate.* The sooner she showed some proficiency in this silly game, the sooner she could get back to her sulfur dioxide analyses—an activity sure to keep her pulse rate down.

The first pitch arced between them. She swung—and missed. The ball bounced to the ground and rolled off behind her.

"It's all right." Garrick held up his mitt. "But try keeping your eyes open when you swing."

She threw him a narrow-eyed look, retrieved the ball, and tossed it to him. She bent her knees and waited for the next pitch. She caught a piece of it, but it bounced foul.

"Better." Garrick ran for the ball and scooped it up in his mitt. "Try holding your swing until the ball's a little closer."

A dozen pitches later, Garrick stopped criticizing and changed the topic of conversation. "So," he said, winding up to throw a pitch, "are you all ready for the champagne brunch on Sunday?"

"What's there to think about?" She bent her knees in readiness. The brunch was just another one of the many social events she and Garrick had been invited to over the past weeks. Always a strain, she avoided thinking about those things until they were upon her. "It's just another party, interrupting crush."

"Ever the working bee."

She swung at the pitch, missing it completely. She glared at him, daring him to say anything, then retrieved the ball.

"Actually," he continued, "I was wondering what you planned to wear."

"Really, Garrick." She tossed him the ball. "Don't tell me you're worried we'll clash."

"Humor me, Amanda. What do you plan to wear?"

She shrugged. "Probably my bronze silk."

He paused in his windup. "You can't wear that."

"Why not?"

"You wore it to the Mountain Label anniversary party."

She dropped the tip of the bat to the ground and leaned on it, lifting one hand to her hip. She knew her wardrobe was thin—when she took this job, she hadn't planned on three major social events a week during the height of crush—but the fact that a man had noticed her lack of variety was embarrassing. "What's with this sudden interest in my wardrobe, Kane?"

"You've already worn that bronze dress, and you also wore that red suit twice—last night at the wine tasting, and earlier, at the Vintner's luncheon. Not that I minded. You're a knockout in red." He tugged on his baseball cap, grinning. "But you're in the public eye now. You can't be wearing the same thing twice in one season."

"You've been reading too much Emily Post." She bent her knees and took her stance. "Keep your mind on baseball and throw me that thing."

He prepared to throw. "I can't have my winemaster wearing retreads, Amanda."

"Retreads?!"

"I'll just have to give you a clothing allowance."

"I'll pass." She waved her bat. "Try getting it over the plate, Kane."

"You can't pass." He sighted down the line to the batter's box. "Tomorrow I'm not letting you on this winery unless you show me receipts from at least two major department stores in San Francisco."

She glared at him as he wound up. "Is that an order?"

"Yes."

The ball made an arc toward her. Amanda glared at it, pursing her lips, using all the strength in her arms to swing the bat. The bat and ball connected with a hollow crack. The ball zoomed away, straight down the middle—smack into Garrick's midriff.

The air rushed out of his lungs with a loud whoosh. He clutched his stomach—and the ball—and fell flat on his back into the dust.

"Garrick?!"

She dropped the bat with a clatter and raced toward him, skidding to her knees in a cloud of soot. The Yankee cap had fallen off his head. His eyes were squeezed shut. She touched his chest, searching for blood, for some visible sign of injury. The ball fell out of his fingers and rolled along the ground.

"Garrick!" She tapped his cheek. "Are you all right?"

He turned his head and blinked one eye open. His face was still squeezed in a grimace. "This . . . wouldn't be a subtle request . . . for a raise, would it?"

She yanked his arms away and pulled up his sweatshirt. A faint red welt rose on his flat, tense belly where the ball had hit. "I didn't break any of your ribs or anything, did I?"

"Feels like I got hit with a hunk of lead." He winced as he sat up on his elbows and peered down at the angry mark. "At least I know what to do next May . . ." He grimaced as he sat up, fully, "when the team is down in the ninth."

"This isn't funny." She drew her brows together, watching him as he shifted his position until he sat comfortably. He spread his hand over his chest. She had swung that bat hard—and hit that ball squarely—and she knew enough about the laws of physics to know that the ball had hit him with just as much force. She took his arm and ducked her head under it, determined to get him up and into her pickup truck. "Come on." She placed her hand on his opposite shoulder, prepared to heave all two-hundred-odd pounds of him to his feet. "We're going to the hospital—"

"Amanda, that isn't necessary."

"Kane, don't be a fool. I'm not going to let you play macho and waddle around this place with a set of broken ribs."

"Listen, slugger," he continued, resisting her efforts to get him up, "you wielded that bat like a true Viking, but I didn't get hit hard enough to break any ribs."

She looked at him suspiciously, seeing the beads of sweat on his upper lip, the dust clinging to his hair.

"Really." He lifted up his cut-off sweatshirt and poked around the welt. "See? I'm not wincing too badly."

She sank back down on her calves, letting go of his arm. She searched his eyes until she was sure he was telling the truth.

He smiled then, a wide grin, and knocked her gently on her chin with his fist. "It's all right." His knuckles lingered on her throat. "But it's nice to know you care."

She wanted to wrap her arms around his neck, kiss him in the dusty driveway until she was sure he was fine. By the look in his eyes, he wouldn't mind a bit. She knew *she* wouldn't; the adrenaline still pumped in her blood, now joined by other chemicals—those pesky hormones that had been kept constantly alert since the day she met Garrick Kane.

Suddenly, she realized that they were all alone in the driveway. The cellar rats were long gone. She could smell open fires and roasting meat coming from the migrant workers' camp, but that lay clear on the other side of the winery. A cool evening breeze picked up, rustling the leaves of the oak trees by the wine cellar, rippling over the vineyards, and chilling the sweat gathering between her breasts. She breathed in the fresh air and smelled the heat of him, so close to her.

She could kiss him now. She wanted to kiss him. She wanted to feel his arms, warm and strong, around her. She stood up abruptly, stumbling away from him.

"No playing wounded hero, Kane." She wiped her knees free of dirt, hoping the growing dusk hid her reaction. "Next time, duck when I swing."

His laughter rang in her ears as she walked numbly back to the batter's box. It was madness to even consider making love with Garrick Kane. He was not part of her well-made plans—he was an unpredictable, uncontrollable, *disruptive* element in the quiet world she had made for herself. If she succumbed to him, she'd be risking her independence, her autonomy, the peace of mind she had curried since the day her father died.

But over the past weeks, Amanda had come to one undeniable conclusion.

No matter how hard she fought, no matter how much she feared the consequences, she was falling wildly, irrationally, irrevocably in love with Garrick Kane.

Garrick strode up the stairs to Amanda's condominium and pressed the doorbell. He tugged uncomfortably on the black lapels of his tuxedo jacket, feeling like a teenager picking up his date for the prom. It had been that long since he had been so eager for a date.

The door swung open abruptly. Amanda's face, bare of makeup, appeared around the edge.

"Sorry," she said breathlessly, brushing a lock of hair out of her eyes. "I'm running late."

His gaze rolled over her, from the tangle of her hair to the bare feet peeping out beneath the sleek length of textured blue satin. "Amanda Karlson? Late? There's a first."

"Come in. I just need a few more minutes."

He stepped in. Usually, when he picked her up for these events, she came to the door fully dressed and ready to leave. This was the first time he had entered the hallowed halls of Amanda's home.

"I got caught up in the cellar this afternoon," she explained as she closed the door behind him. "The servicemen didn't do a very good job on that fermentation tank. The temperatures have been quirky all day."

"Something told me that it wasn't Baby Godzilla in Mushroom Land that delayed you." Garrick scanned the living room/dining room area of the condominium, noticing the clear, sterile tabletops, the pillows squared neatly on the mauve-patterned couch, the pile of untouched mail on one edge of a sofa table. "Don't worry about it. We'll just be fashionably late."

"Help yourself to whatever is in the fridge. No beer, I'm afraid, but there might be some wine."

He openly admired her cobalt-blue dress, which covered her curves sleekly from neck to hem. As she passed him, heading toward a hall, his gaze followed. He caught sight of her back and made a muffled noise of surprise.

She glanced at him over her shoulder, smiling. "Hey, I thought you might be getting used to wine . . ." Her smile died when she saw the direction of his gaze. She twisted, looked down at her own back, then up again at him, expectantly.

Every red corpuscle in his body surged to one very sensitive, now semi-engorged spot. Speechless, he stared at her naked back—and naked it was, bare and narrow, curving in sweetly at the waist and flaring out to slim hips. No tan lines marred the pale, pearly beauty of her skin. When she twisted, the muscles moved in sleek confluence, like muscles rippling under the coat of a wildcat.

Nervously, she gathered a length of the textured satin in one hand. "It's too much, isn't it?"

He swallowed drily, trying to maintain some sort of equilibrium. "You've never worn anything like *that,* Amanda."

She shrugged, sending the hem of the dress swaying against her legs, showing even more skin. "I've never been to the Georges Duchamp charity ball, either."

"Are you sure that thing is safe?"

"Maggie assured me it was." She ran a hand over the hem, pressing it against her skin. Then she dropped the balled satin in her hand and headed toward a hall. "I'll change—"

"No, don't." He stepped toward her, stopping as she stopped. "It's stunning. You're stunning." He shoved his hands into his pockets. "Don't change."

"Are you sure?"

"Yes." He nodded toward the kitchen, an open alcove abutting the living room/dining room area. "Do you have anything more potent than wine in there? Whiskey maybe? Moonshine?" He glanced once more at the sheath of blue satin and balled his hands into fists. "Valium?"

"Sorry, Kane." Her lips twitched, and for a moment, he swore he saw the devil in her eyes. "The hardest thing in this house is wine."

Not right at this moment.

He should be nominated for sainthood, he thought as she turned and strode down the hall. The sight of her naked back nearly pushed him over the edge—his patience and control were already stretched to the breaking point. Every social event they attended, every impromptu basketball game, where she pranced around in shorts and a sweaty, clinging T-shirt, every single moment in her presence was a strain. He didn't know how much longer he could joke with and laugh and tease her without dragging her into his arms and making wild, passionate love to her.

Tonight, he thought, digging his fingernails into his palms. There would be dancing tonight at the gala. He had been looking forward to this event for a full week. Come hell or high water, he intended to dance with Amanda Karlson. And later, much later, in some private spot, he intended to kiss her good night—and see whether the softening he had witnessed these past weeks was more than just friendship.

He wandered toward the kitchen and opened the fridge, searching for something to chill his ardor. Nothing but a bottle of diet soda, a few condiments, a couple of bottles of wine, and a scattering of fruit littered the inside of the fridge. He decided to pass on the wine. Nothing, absolutely *nothing*, manmade or natural, could wipe the sight of Amanda's bare back from his mind.

Instead, he searched through the cabinets for a glass, filled it with ice, and poured in water from the tap. He thought wryly that pouring it down his trousers would be a more effective way of chilling his passion, but he opted instead to drink it, hoping the cool liquid would ice his blood before she returned and discovered what a pointed effect she had on his libido.

He strode around the room, waiting for his pulse rate to slow. The condo looked more like a hotel room than a home. No crumbs littered the antique dining-room table. All the chairs were drawn neatly in. As he wandered over the sand-colored wall-to-wall carpeting toward the dining room, he noticed a three-week-old TV guide on the glass coffee table and the wilted plants hanging in the windows. The only personal touch in the room was a gathering of photos atop a cherrywood sofa table.

He placed the empty water glass on the coffee table and sank a knee into the cushions on the floral couch, peering at the scattered photos in silver frames. Some of the photos were old, sepia-tinted, of unsmiling brides and grooms. Others were more modern. Two were of women who looked like Amanda—sisters, Garrick concluded—in graduation dress. One photo, the one in the largest frame and in the center of the collection, caught and held his attention.

He reached for it. It was a family photo, slightly crinkled and torn in one corner. Three towheaded girls, gangly in early adolescence, grinned and leaned back against a large wine barrel. Garrick immediately recognized Amanda as the eldest, despite her straight, girlish figure, the braces, and the smile that held no trace of coolness or tension. No one in the photo wore any shoes, and they all displayed their grape juice–stained feet with pride. The parents—almost as fair as the children—sat upon the barrel, dressed in old overalls, hugging one another, smiling broadly into the camera. Garrick peered at her father, seeing the humor crinkling around his eyes, and remembered what Amanda had said: *He would have liked you. He was very . . . playful.*

The photo was a single frozen instance of pure happiness.

"I'm the ugly duckling on the right."

He looked up as she entered the room. She had swept her hair up off the curve of her neck and darkened her lashes with mascara. She clutched a tube of lipstick in one hand and a pair of high-heeled black pumps in the other.

"I could tell by the legs."

She frowned at him and glanced around the room. "Did you see my purse around here?"

"It's on the dining-room table." He pointed to the beaded black bag, hidden from her view by a ceramic centerpiece. "Was this photo taken on that farm in Massachusetts?"

"A-yup," she said. She tossed the shoes on the floor and wiggled into them, then walked to the dining-room table. "We had just finished getting all the new wine into that keg. It was our last harvest. My father died a few months later."

He looked at her sharply. She avoided his eyes and dropped her lipstick into the purse. She rummaged through the bag, as if she had just told him the time of day and not that her father had died so young. But he had become an expert at reading Amanda and he saw that her hands were trembling.

The dam is crumbling, he thought. These glimpses of her past were rare and uncommon. They teased him. He wanted to know more—he wanted to know exactly what made Amanda Karlson tick. He looked down at the smiling man, robust and full of health. Then he peered more closely at the image of the man's eldest daughter. "Amanda . . . You couldn't have been more than thirteen years old."

"Just fourteen." She pulled two glittering earrings out of her bag. "The neighbor who took the picture gave it to my mother at my father's funeral."

"I'm sorry." He knew how trite the words sounded, for he had heard them a hundred times not so long ago, but he didn't know how else to express his sympathy. "He looks as healthy as an ox in this picture."

"He was. It was an accident." She slipped the post of one of the earrings through her pierced ear. Her voice wavered. "He was on an icy road, and a truck coming in the opposite direction lost control . . . It was no one's fault."

Something squeezed around Garrick's heart. He couldn't imagine what it would have been like to lose a parent so young—and so abruptly. Hell, he was thirty-five and still struggling to get over the death of his brother. Amanda had lost a father before she was out of braces.

Then he remembered something she had told him at Cedar Ridge. The pieces were beginning to fall into place. "After your father died . . . is that when your family lost the farm?"

"Not long after." She fumbled with the other earring. She seemed to be having great difficulty finding the hole in her earlobe. "My father lingered in the hospital for almost a month. Most of the insurance money we received went to pay his medical bills, and there was nothing left to pay the mortgage."

And so you lost your father, and your farm, and your world, didn't you, Amanda?

Garrick rubbed a thumb over the silver frame, staring into Amanda's past and beginning to fully understand her for the first time. "What did you all do, after the farm was gone?"

"My mother worked. I worked." She tugged nervously on the earrings. "I could probably set a record with the number of jobs I held—fast-food restaurants, late shifts at movie houses, morning shifts on an assembly line—whatever I could do to keep us from eating all our meals at the church."

Christ, he thought. He hadn't realized . . . No wonder she clung so fiercely to her career. All these years had passed, and Amanda still hadn't stopped working.

"My mother is living in upstate New York now," she said, her voice falsely bright. "She remarried a few years ago—a doctor."

"I'm glad to hear there's a happy ending."

"She deserves a little happiness." She plucked at the beads on her black bag. "On Sunday evenings, my sisters and I used to watch old black-and-white movies on TV. I used to scoff when the heroines died so conveniently of grief. But after Dad died, and I saw Mom . . . I didn't laugh at them anymore."

Looking at her, Garrick thought that without the armor of steel she usually wore, Amanda was as soft and vulnerable as a turtle without its shell. His whole body leaned toward her. He wanted to take her in his arms. As if sensing his intentions, she looked up at him and started.

"That's all past," she said swiftly, snapping her bag shut. "We all managed to find our way in the world." Clutching the purse beneath her elbow, she headed toward the door. "My sister Rachel is a photographer, a bit of a bohemian, but she does all right. Karen is married and has two children and owns a farm in Connecticut."

"And you're winemaster at Cedar Ridge."

She opened the door and stood bathed in the evening light. "A winemaker who's going to miss her first Georges Duchamp Charity Gala Ball if her boss doesn't stop asking so many questions."

"Heaven forbid." He placed the photo back in the middle of the sofa table, knowing that her confession had reached its end. She had revealed more to him in the past ten minutes than she had in the past ten weeks; he would not spoil it by insisting on hearing more. "I suppose we should rush. We might actually miss the antics of a dozen hired Italian acrobats, or maybe the cameo appearance of some Hollywood starlet."

"I believe the entertainment tonight is the landing of a dozen red hot air balloons at sunset." Though her gleaming lips stretched in a smile, the shadow of her sadness still lingered. "You're becoming a cynic, Kane. This isn't the Big Apple. What else can we do for excitement up here?"

"Shovel grapes. Hunt for rattlesnakes in the vineyards. Stick needles in our eyes." He paused on the landing outside the condo as she walked down the stairs, gazing at the fantastic length of that naked back at a new angle. "Personally, I think I have all the excitement I need with me."

She glanced at him over her shoulder, one brow lifting. "This dress is your fault, Kane. You forced me to go shopping. I don't always make rational decisions under pressure."

"I like it when you're irrational." He kept his gaze on the twitch of her near-naked hips as he pulled the car keys out of his pocket and opened the door for her. "I just don't know if I want to give the entire male population of Napa Valley a chance to see the lovely Amanda Karlson so exposed.''

"Get in and drive.'' She slipped into the front seat and looked up at him, all sparkling green eyes. ''And keep your eyes on the road, hmm?''

Hours later, the Georges Duchamp gala rocked at full swing. A Dixie band played trumpet-squealing, partner-swinging music and half the party crowded onto the parquet dancing floor laid out beneath a tent in an open field beside the white stucco winery. Discreet waiters in blinding white tuxedos hovered around the perimeter, refolding napkins and refilling half-empty wineglasses with the sticky dessert wine.

Garrick leaned against a garlanded post in the shadows, took a sip of the sweet white wine, and forced himself to swallow. His gaze followed Amanda as she worked the room. She floated from one table to another, pressing the flesh, making contacts with innumerable restaurateurs, wine distributors, wine writers, and other powerhouses in the business. At one point, she bent over to speak to someone sitting at one of the tables. Garrick tightened his grip on his wineglass. A cluster of men who stood behind her teetered en masse in one direction, then the other, straining to see down the gaping back of her dress. Garrick had spent the entire night holding his breath, waiting for that dress to gape the wrong way and reveal too much of her pale, pearly flesh. He felt like standing behind her, shielding all that nakedness from the sight of other men's eyes.

He could sure use a cold, frosty beer right about now. There were too many other men's eyes on Amanda and it was driving him crazy. Some tall blond had been trailing her for a good twenty minutes, regaining her attention at every opportunity. Yet Garrick couldn't say a thing—and he certainly couldn't go and pull her away without a damned good reason. These winery fêtes were becoming nothing more than frustrating exercises in self-control. He couldn't be seen with his hands on a beer or with his hands on Amanda.

At least he could have the beer when he got home.

The band broke out into a bluesy selection, something slow and smoky. People filtered off the dance floor, leaving only swaying couples behind. Garrick glanced enviously at the floor, then with growing intent on Amanda. He had been waiting for an opportunity to dance with her all night—that was as good an excuse as any to get her away from that blond.

He put his glass down resolutely, then wove through the tables, keeping his gaze on Amanda so he wouldn't be stopped by any of the people he knew in the crowd. She perched her curvy little bottom on the edge of a chair and gazed up at the blond with a polite social smile on her face. Garrick wondered if the man was too stupid or too frightened to ask her to dance. Her gaze flickered to Garrick as he approached, and he saw the light of relief in her green eyes.

"Excuse me." Garrick reached for her arm and pulled her up. He smiled blandly into the startled man's face. "I've got to steal my winemaker away for a while. You don't mind, do you?"

He didn't wait for an answer. He turned and led her through the crowd, squiring her onto the dance floor, not giving her an opportunity to object. He swung around to face her only when they were nestled deep within the swarm of swaying couples.

She held out her arms. "Thank God you came."

"You looked like a damsel in distress." He took her

hand, pleased at her easy acquiescence. "Who was that guy?"

"I forget. After thirty or forty introductions, I start to lose track. He's a winemaker." Her glittering earrings dangled against her neck as he wrapped his arm around her waist and pulled her against him. "If he had said one more word about yeast strains in Pinot Noir fermentation, I was going to *scream.*"

"You're safe with me." His fingers had nowhere to go but against her warm, naked flesh. He felt the indentation of her spine and the flex of her lean muscles, the smooth heat of her body. He resisted the urge to plunge his hand deep beneath the hem, to discover exactly what kind of sexy, next-to-nothing lingerie she wore beneath this dress. "I promise not to mention yeast whatever for the duration of this dance."

She looked up at him, raising one brow as if she could read his mind. "Seems to me I just jumped out of the frying pan and into the fire."

He grinned. "I deserve a reward for riding in on my white charger."

"Just make sure you keep your hands in sight, buster."

"Amanda, in this dress, that's not asking for much."

She grimaced. "I never should have worn it. Every time I turn around some man is leaning over me like the Tower of Pisa." She shivered deliciously, and her skin rippled beneath his hand. "A forensic chemist would have a field day dusting my back off for fingerprints."

"I'm not surprised." With subtle pressure against her lower back, he drew her closer, tormenting himself with the feel of her thighs brushing his legs, stifling the urge to bury his face in her hair. "Any excuse to touch a beautiful woman will do."

"Including dancing?"

His grin widened. "Hell, I've been looking forward to this all month."

"Well, try not to let it show." She inched a fraction away from him, a smile tugging at her lips. "Sadie Cello has probably already marked me as a tart for wearing this dress. She'll be looking for an indiscretion. Finding my boss's hand down my dress would be a nice tidbit for next week's column."

"Hey, haven't I been the perfect gentleman around you at these things?"

"So far you've been remarkably well behaved."

"So far?" He tightened his grip around her back, staring at her incredulously, wondering if she knew that he was one flirtatious remark away from burying his lips in the fragrant hollow right behind her ear. "Don't you trust me yet?"

She lifted a brow. "So the wolf asked the sheep."

"You're no sheep." He jerked his head toward the crowd in general. "You're herding in business like a professional wrangler. There isn't a distributor in the place who'll forget your name tomorrow. I think the dress was pure brilliance."

"Is that why you're dancing with me, Garrick? Because of a job well done?"

She tilted her head, one glittering earring lying against her throat, her eyes sparkling with a bright, reckless light. Every blood cell in his body rushed to his loins. Her lips looked soft, moist, inviting, still red with lipstick. He wanted to kiss it all off. He wanted to pull every pin out of the neat French twist and watch her hair fall over her bare shoulders. He wished the crowd would disappear and leave him alone with this woman and the music, just for a moment, just long enough for him to kiss her thoroughly. Their bodies brushed one against the other, rubbing together like dry sticks, giving off sparks.

Then her smile wavered and the twinkle in her eyes dulled to a hesitant gleam. "Oh, God. Don't answer that." Her gaze flickered nervously to the couples around them. "I've had one too many glasses of fine vintage wine tonight."

"*In vino veritas.*" He held her tighter as she tried to gently pull away. "I'll slake your curiosity, Amanda. There isn't a man in this room right now who isn't looking at me, green with envy."

"You're imagining things." She opened her hand, then closed it again, slipping her fingers down deeper between his. "Personally, I think they've all just eaten too much of the steak tartare."

He laughed. Something burst in his chest—something bright and joyous and rejuvenating. He hadn't felt this lighthearted since long before Dominick's death. He squeezed her tight against him, resisting for propriety's sake the urge to sweep her up and spin her around in his arms, instead giving in to the laughter bubbling up like champagne in his chest. She was a tonic to him; he wondered if she knew it. He spread his fingers over her bare back, grinning, while his mind raced ahead. Tonight, he thought. God willing, he would finally make love to Amanda tonight.

"Take me to Cedar Ridge first, will you, Garrick? I want to check on that fermentation tank, in case anything went wrong."

Garrick nodded mutely and veered the Saab up the

mountain road toward Cedar Ridge. Amanda had made the request with her usual calm, but he could tell she was nervous. She sat stiffly in the passenger's seat, toying with her bag, rolling her fingers over the beads and flipping it over and over in her lap. He wondered if she really had to go to Cedar Ridge at one in the morning—or if, as he hoped, she had used the request as an excuse to be alone with him for the night.

His body ached for her. He forced himself to remember that beneath her cool veneer lay a frightened fourteen-year-old girl, bereft of a father, bereft of a home, bereft of all the security she had ever known—and frightened to death of ever depending on anyone else for her happiness. He had to move carefully, slowly, easing her into this ultimate intimacy, so she would know that he wouldn't hurt her—that all he wanted to do was to make her believe in magic again.

He parked the Saab in front of the main house. A full moon hung high in the sky, casting a silvery sheen over the vineyard, illuminating the fog that edged over the ridge and spilled down into the valley like wisps of fine cotton. She let herself out of the car before he could walk around to her side. He walked up the stairs to the veranda and fumbled with his house keys, then opened the door into blackness.

He heard her footsteps crunching in the packed earth as she headed around the winery. "Garrick, I'll just go around to the cellar and check on things—"

"Come into the house first." He walked to the edge of the veranda and looked at her, poised and hesitant, her satin dress gleaming like silver in the moonlight. "I'll change out of this monkey suit and I'll help you if there's a problem."

"I'll be fine—"

"Amanda, you'll ruin that very expensive dress if you start climbing on chairs in that cellar."

She smoothed her hands over her hips, then shrugged and walked toward him. He smelled the faint scent of her elegant perfume as she brushed by him and entered the main house. He closed the door behind her and took her elbow so she wouldn't stumble in the dark.

He felt her start, but he ignored it. He led her into the kitchen. Moonlight spilled in through the windows, and he decided not to turn on the lights. He released her and walked to the fridge, tugging his tuxedo jacket off his shoulders and pulling his bow tie until the ends were free.

"I've been dying for a beer all night." Opening the fridge, he pulled out a bottle. "Can I get you anything?"

"No. I'm fine."

She dropped her bag on the counter and hugged her elbows close to her body. He cracked the beer open and lifted it to his lips, but the flow of the icy liquid did nothing to stifle his growing desire. She looked so beautiful leaning against the counter with the pale moonlight washing over her, the satin clinging to her breasts, to the sleek curve of her hips, the bent curve of one knee . . .

The bottle clattered on the table. He crossed the distance that separated them and placed his hands on the counter on either side of her hips, trapping her. His voice fought its way through his constricted throat. "Did you really come here to check the fermentation temperatures, Amanda?"

She parted her lips and drew in a deep breath. She stared somewhere in the middle of his chest. She didn't struggle—she didn't pull away—she stood as still as stone, as if she was afraid to move.

So he lifted one hand and pulled the pins out of her hair, letting them tinkle, one by one, onto the counter, some falling over the edge to the floor. Her hair swished heavily over her shoulders, swooping down like smooth, brushed flax, shimmering in the pale light. He had always wanted to do this, to see her hair, just once, unbound around her shoulders. When the last pin fell to the counter, he buried both hands deep in her warm tresses and gently pulled her head back so she could no longer avoid his eyes.

"There's no one here, Amanda, but you and me." His heart pounded like thunder in his chest, for she was all softness—her eyes open and moist, her lips gleaming and swollen, begging for a kiss. He lowered his head and brushed her lips gently—a butterfly's kiss—the first taste of paradise. "God, Amanda . . ." His voice broke. "Don't fight me tonight. Don't fight yourself."

He took her lower lip between his, suckled it, tasting the vestiges of sweet wine. He released the tender flesh and then gently attacked her upper lip. She moaned, a quiet sound in the silent kitchen, and his heart raced as he felt her fingers climbing up his shirt, winding around his neck, burrowing in the crisp curls of his hair.

It was all he needed. He pulled her close, wrapped his arms around her, then swept his hands down, down, over all the bare skin once forbidden to him. She arched her back like a cat, driving her body close to his, opening her mouth to his. He rubbed the calloused heel of one hand down the indentation of her spine, no longer stopping at the low hem of her dress. He slipped his hand lower—and jolted in surprise as he realized that all she wore beneath the satin was the briefest of G-strings.

He made a noise against her mouth, undefinable, raw and primitive, then delved deeper beneath the hem of her dress, cupping her firm, rounded buttocks in his hands.

He lifted her high against the cabinet, so their faces were level, so he could look into her eyes.

"Say you'll make love with me, Amanda."

There was a moment of strained silence. Her head fell back as he nipped her throat, and she said one single word:

"*Yes.*"

EIGHT

The minute Amanda opened her lips to Garrick, she welcomed him with abandon. Weeks of frustration, weeks of suppressed desire rose up and inundated her, sweeping away her inhibitions, overwhelming every last trace of doubt. She had made her decision—she had taken the risk—and now nothing, *nothing*, was going to come between her and this feast of forbidden fruit.

So she feasted. She kissed him, hungrily, trying to satisfy all her yearnings, so long suppressed. She couldn't touch him fully enough, thoroughly enough, and she struggled to express the emotions that tumbled inside her. She buried her fingers deep in his thick, silky hair, she pressed her body flat against his, reveling in the hardness of him, the muscular planes and angles so different from those of her body. She felt the rumbling in his chest as he groaned; she felt the vibrations against the sensitive tips of her breasts. She yearned to be a part of him, to draw him deep into her woman's body and give him a man's pleasure. Every fiber of her being screamed *yield, yield,* and she did, giving in to every wordless request, answering the merest touch of his lips, aching deep down inside for something greater than the mere union of their bodies.

She couldn't speak—she could hardly breathe. He kneaded her hips gently, his fingers scraping tender skin. Through his trousers she felt the hardness of his arousal, nudging against her. Silently, she cursed the tight, sleek lines of the dress—it restricted her, when she no longer wanted to be restricted. With his rough hands holding her so intimately, his lips ravaging her throat, she felt desired—utterly—yet she ached for a deeper and more intimate passion.

The moonlight flooded over them, bathing them in silver. She clung to the thinnest thread of sanity as his cheek, slightly bewhiskered, scraped against her throat. She cradled his head as he kissed through the satin, as he nudged his chin against her breasts. He released her hips and settled her back on her feet, only to grasp the edges of her satin dress behind her shoulders and yank it down over her shoulders, and farther, over her elbows, until her breasts were exposed to his gaze, and then to his touch . . . then to his kiss.

She clutched his muscled upper arms as his hot mouth closed over one pink, puckered nipple. She squeezed her eyes shut as a tremor shot right down to her toes, then back again, reverberating through her body. She wanted to hug him, to draw her closer, but the bunched satin of her dress restricted her movement even more than before. She struggled to pull her arms out of the long sleeves as he suckled and nipped and kissed her breasts, until finally, exultantly, she drew her hands out of the tubes of binding satin and thrust her fingers through his hair.

Suddenly, he released her. He swung an arm beneath her knees and lifted her in his arms.

"Upstairs." His voice was ragged, his hair mussed, his eyes like blue lightning. "Tonight, I'm going to make love to you properly, Amanda. Not on a table. Not against a counter. And not on my kitchen floor."

He left the kitchen, strode down the hall, and climbed the stairs to his bedroom. She buried her head in the nook of his neck, trying to catch her breath. She had never felt like this with any man—she had never wanted to feel like this, so out of control of her own senses—but since the first time she saw Garrick it seemed her senses and emotions had reeled utterly out of her power. Now, for this brief moment in time, she allowed herself this heady freedom. It was like teetering on the edge of a cliff—but she was not frightened. Garrick was here, Garrick would not hurt her, Garrick would hold her tight while she fell.

He nudged the door to his bedroom open with one shoulder, then kicked it shut behind him. The moonlight spilled over the unmade bed, still rumpled from when he had slept in it the night before. He settled her feet on the plush carpet, then looked at her while the satin dress sagged around her hips.

He wanted her. She saw it in the way his chest rose and fell rapidly, in the way he looked at her, all fire and passion. She approached him, spread her fingers over the cotton of his shirt, then undid the buttons, one by one.

"I've dreamt about doing this to you." She hardly recognized her own voice, it sounded so deep and sultry. She spread the edges of his shirt, exposing the well-muscled pectorals, the sculpted ripples of his abdomen. She pressed her lips in the warm indentation of his chest. "I tried not to, but . . ."

"Don't think about that—not tonight." He slid his thumbs beneath the satin clinging to her hips and, with one gentle tug, let the material swoosh to a puddle at her feet. The wisp of undergarment followed. "Tonight, you're not a chemist, you're not my employee, you're more than my friend. You're a woman. *My* woman."

She stood against him, utterly naked but for the glittering faux emerald earrings dangling against her neck, her lips pressed in his chest, her lashes tangling with his chest hair. *My woman.* She didn't want to be anyone's anything—she didn't want to depend on anyone—but his words sounded like sweet music nonetheless. She curled her fingers into his shirt.

He lifted her up against his body so that her face was level with his. He stared at her, all of her, from her loose, moonlit hair, to the place between them where their bodies met.

He kissed the tip of her nose, then brushed his lips over hers. "I've wanted you for so long."

The sheets felt cool against her back as he laid her on them. She closed her eyes as his weight covered her. Nothing separated the heat of their bodies but the thin material of his trousers. She fought to hold onto sanity for just one moment longer; the rational part of her would not let go until one last issue was addressed and settled, before she gave herself up to passion.

"Garrick—" Her breath caught as he nudged her legs apart with one knee. "I'm not . . . protected."

He brushed her hair off her face. "I'll take care of it. I'll take care of everything."

She knew it was true, someplace deep inside her, she

knew Garrick would make sure she was safe. They were friends first, only now becoming lovers—a potent, dangerous transition, but there was more than a little madness in this lovemaking. Madness! Her world had been thrown into chaos since she had met him. This was never supposed to happen to her—she had spent a lifetime making sure it didn't.

Tomorrow, tomorrow she would let herself think, she told herself. Tonight, with Garrick's warm body atop hers, with his breath mingling with hers, with his tongue stirring magic between her lips, she was capable only of feeling.

He began a new assault on her naked body. She clung to his bare back—for he had tossed his shirt into the shadows—while he kissed down, over her throat, pausing for a while to suckle on her breasts, to draw the pink tips between his lips and to mold each breast in his rough palms. Every caress spiraled downward, deep into her body, knotting her abdomen into tenseness. He released her breasts only to spread kisses through the hollow of her abdomen, while his fingers trailed over her ribs. He discovered the pucker of her navel, and explored still lower.

He nudged her legs open with his shoulders and kissed her. She arched her back, squeezed her eyes shut, and curled her fists into the sheets. Garrick relentlessly continued his caresses, forcing her thighs wide, urging her to feel the joy that came from giving a part of herself up to him, the pleasure that came from losing control. She succumbed. She had no choice, for he continued until she lay breathless, trembling, her eyes closed, her entire body throbbing.

He stopped, but she knew instinctively it was only for the moment. He tossed his trousers into the darkness and opened a drawer beside his bed. The moonlight cast his back in granite, but this was no statue—this was flesh and blood, and she knew it for sure when he settled back on the bed and tore open the foil packet.

She opened herself to him as she had dreamed of doing for so long. At this moment, she wanted him to possess her—*needed* him to possess her—not only in body, but also in heart and soul. It was as if all the layers of armor she had spent so many years building had slipped away, one by one, leaving nothing protecting her but hope. And trust.

She tilted her hips, eager, granting him entry, and then he slid inside her, where he belonged.

Where he belonged.

His breath heated her hair just above her ear as he lay, still, their bodies joined. "Amanda . . ."

Her fingers trembled against his back. She had never felt so complete, so whole, as she did this moment, pressing her lips against his shoulder, listening to the pounding of his heart, feeling that part of him throbbing deep inside her. She had finally found some missing piece of herself.

He moved, poised above her slightly on his elbows. She was conscious of more than just the length of him inside her. She felt the slickness of sweat on his back, the heat of his skin, the salty taste of his neck, and the musky smell of their lovemaking. He murmured things against her ear, but she was beyond comprehension, she was someplace bright and wonderful, someplace high and full of stars.

Later, much later, she languidly blinked her eyes open and found herself covered with a sheet, her nose pressed against Garrick's neck, while he combed his fingers through the tangles in her hair.

He was still holding her.

She closed her eyes and lost herself again, this time in blissful sleep.

Amanda woke slowly. She shifted her position to avoid the light that fell across her closed eyes. She heard beyond the walls of the room the muffled chirping of birds, and she knew that morning had come. Still, she lazed about, stretching her arms far above her head, feeling all warm and cozy at the core, reveling in a rare sense of peaceful contentment.

She pressed her cheek against the cool pillow, breathing in a spicy, familiar fragrance. Memory returned— lots of memory—of heated kisses and steamy, early-morning lovemaking. She curled her legs up, her body tingling with heat. She reached across the bed and found it empty.

She blinked her eyes open and stared at the linens twisted and tangled into knots. She eased herself up on her elbows, scanning the room.

Garrick was nowhere in sight.

She ran a hand through her tangled hair, wondering where he could have gone so early in the morning. She glanced at the bronze alarm clock and found it face-down on the nightstand. She stretched across the bed and turned the timepiece upright, then gasped when she saw it was past eleven o'clock.

She clasped the sheet to her breasts, suddenly wide awake. She had ordered two cellar rats to come in today and finish the racking of the Chardonnay. They were due to arrive hours ago . . . and she was lying in her boss's bed, as naked as a newborn, sleeping away the morning.

She searched around the room and realized all she

had to wear was her satin dress, which lay in a shimmering blue pile near the door. She kicked away the linens and shimmied to the side of the bed, reaching instead for Garrick's white tuxedo shirt lying on the pine-green carpet. She slipped her arms into the sleeves and buttoned it, rolling the cuffs up until they hung around her elbows, trying to ignore the spicy scent of his cologne wafting up from the fibers. She had a change of clothes in the cellar, but there was no way for her to get to them unless she wanted to pad naked across the driveway—or waltz into the cellar decked in nothing but Garrick's shirt. She had to find Garrick and somehow, someway, have him get her clothes out of the cellar without any of the rats noticing.

She started as the door squealed open. Garrick backed his way in, carrying a wicker tray laden with coffee and orange juice and steaming scrambled eggs.

"Garrick!"

He turned around and leaned back against the door as he noticed her skimpy, gaping attire. "Sweet Mother Mary, I'll never wear that shirt again."

"You've got to help me." She pranced to the window and peered out anxiously through the slats of the blinds. "I've got some clothes in the cellar—"

"And there they'll stay." His smoky blue gaze swept over her as he walked across the room and placed the tray on the nightstand beside the bed. "Clothes are forbidden today—except maybe that shirt."

"This isn't time for games, Garrick." For a moment she lost her train of thought, for he wore only a pair of boxer shorts, and the sight of his half-naked body in the morning light was almost too much for her to ignore, especially after the intimacies of the evening. But there was something more pressing, something that had to be attended to immediately. "Do you know how late it is?"

He crawled across the bed, then sat on her side and held out his hand. "Later than you've ever slept, I imagine."

"We've got a problem. I told two cellar rats to come in this morning. They're probably waiting for me, right now in the cellar."

"I told them to go home." He took her hand, tugged her closer, then clutched her by the waist, burying his face in her abdomen, and searching between the buttons of his shirt for her navel. "It's Sunday, Amanda. A day of rest, remember?"

Rest was the last thing on her mind as his hot tongue found flesh beneath the cotton. She gripped his head, running her fingers through his mussed hair. "Garrick . . . I can't think straight when you do that."

"Good."

"Are . . . the rats gone?"

"Um-huh."

"What—" she gasped as he reached behind one knee and pulled it onto the bed, forcing her, spreadeagled, onto his lap. "What did you tell them to make them leave?"

His eyes twinkled as he looked up at her. "I told them you were sprawled across my bed, laid up for the day."

"You *what*—"

He swallowed her squeal of protest with a kiss. She pressed her hands against his shoulders as his unshaven cheek razed her skin. Finally, she struggled free of his kiss and glared down at him.

"That's not funny, Kane. Tell me you're teasing."

"I'm teasing." His grin had all the easy, reckless

charm of a man who had just spent the whole evening making love. "Don't worry, Amanda. They knew you were at the Duchamp gala last night. I told them you were too beat to come in and you called in to tell me to dismiss them for the day."

She looked suspiciously at his heavy-lidded eyes, seductive and very blue in the dim bedroom. "Did they accept it?"

"Without question and with great relief." He wrapped his arms more tightly around her waist, drawing her hips up until she sat squarely on his loins. "There's no one here but you and me. No cellar rats, no distributors, and no damned reporters." He nuzzled in the low, open V of the shirt. "That is what you're afraid of, isn't it?"

"Well . . ." She caught her breath as he nudged the shirt to one side, his bristled cheek scraping the sensitive skin of one breast. She was afraid of something else . . . something she'd have to ask him, and soon. "I was wondering . . . what we were going to do."

"I thought we'd start off with a little breakfast." Nudging the shirt aside with his nose, he found what he was searching for. He rubbed his cheek gently against the tip of her taut nipple. "Then maybe a few table hockey games, a Bogart movie—"

"I didn't mean today," she murmured, her voice shaky from his incessant caresses. "I meant—what are we going to do about this situation?"

"Don't get any ideas about running off." He nipped her neck with his teeth. "I've waited too long for you and I have no intention of letting you go anytime soon."

She wondered why his words made her feel warm

and cherished when she had fought against needing anyone or anything for most of her life.

"We're going to be lovers, Amanda. You're going to sleep in my bed at night and go to work in the wine cellar in the morning."

She lifted a brow at his unquestioning tone of voice. "Is that an order, Mr. Kane?"

"It's negotiable." He closed his lips deliberately over her nipple, drew it into his hot, moist mouth, then released it to cool in the air. "You could work at night and spend all day with me in my bed."

She struggled to catch her breath as he kissed her nipple anew.

"Or maybe we should skip the bed part altogether." His hands slipped beneath the hem of the shirt and slid up her thighs. "I've got a yen to try out that table in the wine cellar again."

She moaned as he curled his fingers around her hips. "This could become very complicated . . ."

"Yes," he murmured, "it could."

"I mean . . . keeping it a secret." She bit her lower lip as Garrick shifted her weight so that she could feel him pressing intimately against her loins. She struggled to resist—for now. She needed to be sure he understood. "You're my boss, Garrick. This would be a ripe plum for Sadie Cello."

"What happens in this room is between you and me." He lay back on the bed, drawing her down atop him. "To the rest of the world, we're just business associates." He slid his hands up over her hips to her waist, squeezing her tight, meeting her gaze. "Is that what you want to hear?"

"Yes." She paused, bit her lower lip, feeling foolish. She didn't want him to think this was a silly quirk.

Suddenly, it was important that he understood—*really* understood. "I . . . I was a cocktail waitress at night while I went to college, Garrick. I put up with a lot of manhandling—literally—just so when I got out of school I would never have to dress in a short skirt and smile for tips again."

His hands lingered on her thighs. "Why would you think you would?"

"Life is sometimes . . . unpredictable." She rarely spoke of the past to anyone, and the words lay awkward on her tongue. "I thought my life would be set once I graduated and found a job, but when I started working for Windsor . . . I noticed that in some ways, men weren't treating me any differently than if I were still taking drink orders. I had to fight, scratch, and claw just to earn respect."

"You did, Amanda—"

"But it could disappear in a moment, don't you see? Napa isn't like anyplace else—the winemaking business is small and close-knit and . . . incestuous. Everyone knows everyone else. It feeds on its own young."

"Amanda—"

"Reputation is everything," she continued swiftly, letting the words spill from her before she lost her nerve. "Gossip can get really ugly—it can ruin a wine-maker. Whether the rumors are true or false, once mud is thrown, some of it always sticks—"

"Trust me, Amanda."

"I've worked too long and fought too hard, Garrick—"

"Trust me." He kissed her quiet, then brushed her hair off her shoulder. "I won't let them start slinging."

He kissed her again, more deeply, and all her logic fled. He understood; he would keep their affair a secret;

she had nothing to fear. . . . Her eyes fluttered closed as he urged her lips open with his tongue. She tasted the warmth of passion on his breath, the vestiges of rich, strong coffee. She spread her hands over his chest, curling her fingers into the crisp hair. Somehow it was different kissing him in daylight, though the room was dim except for the stripes of sunshine bathing the bed. She couldn't hide now—she couldn't pretend that this passion was all moonlight and madness. It was very real. *He* was very real, unshaven, his hair amuss, his eyes still heavy-lidded with sleep, his lean body warm and strong and bare and vibrant, lying fully beneath her.

Her heart turned over in her chest, full of love for him, full of fear. Whatever she had gotten herself into, it was too late to turn back now, for she wanted this man more than she had wanted almost anything else in her life. She *needed* him. Amanda Karlson, who had shunned relationships for years, who had fought and struggled to support herself in a hostile world, had now fallen head over heels in love with her own boss.

She swallowed the sudden lump in her throat and kissed him swiftly, not wanting him to open his eyes and see the terror emblazoned across her face.

He worked the buttons on the shirt until the edges lay free. He pushed them aside and off her shoulders, then ran one rough-palmed hand from her shoulder to her thigh and back again. He broke the kiss, then gently eased her away, until she kneeled astride him. He gazed hungrily at her body, striped with light.

She felt shy, exposed, with the cotton thrust off her shoulders, though in the darkness he had already discovered every inch of her bare flesh.

He looked up at her and cupped one breast in his hand. "You're beautiful, Amanda."

He gently palmed her breast until the pink nipple stood at attention. She ran a trembling finger over his chest, then lower, over the furred ripples of his abdomen, to slip beneath the hem of his boxer shorts. She tugged at the elastic. "You're still wearing clothes."

"You could take them off me."

She slid down until she straddled his thighs, then tugged on the edge of the boxer shorts, drawing them down over his lean hips, exposing him to her gaze. She drew the boxers beneath her thighs, then reached back and tugged on them until he could kick them to the floor. She touched him with both hands, and felt the heated surge of his passion as he throbbed in her grip. She looked at his face and saw the gleam in his blue eyes.

And suddenly, she felt in control again. Power lay beneath her fingers. With a boldness she hadn't known she possessed, she stroked him, softly at first, more firmly as his lean, strong body flexed in response. Later, she leaned down and brushed her tongue against him.

Garrick whispered for her to reach into the drawer. She pulled out one of the packets, ripped it open, and managed, with some nervous laughter, to roll the condom on him. He reached for her and drew her body atop his. The crisp hair of his chest brushed her tender breasts, and the muscles of his abdomen rippled against her stomach—male against female, hardness against softness. Garrick kissed her, hotter than he had ever kissed her, and Amanda squeezed her eyes shut, gasping for breath as his fingers worked their way over her, touching her where she ached the most, coaxing moans from her lips, easing deep inside her until she was ready for him. She drew her knees up close to his body as he pressed against her soft inner thigh, begging entrance.

"Look at me, Amanda."

She responded to his husky command. He guided her hips atop him. She slipped down slowly and blinked her eyes closed at the feel of him, so hard and full. He touched her cheek, urging her to open her eyes again, forcing her to meet the need and desire in his smoky gaze as they joined in the most intimate way.

"The rest of the whole wide world can go right to hell, Amanda." He brushed her hair away from her face. "In this house, you're all mine."

Garrick watched Amanda over the edge of the latest issue of the *Napa Weekly*. She was curled on a kitchen chair like a cat. She methodically toyed with a multicolored cube, rotating its sections, trying to solve the puzzle. A half-eaten cinnamon-apple muffin from her favorite bakery and a cup of strong black coffee lay on the table, cooling.

She had been at it for a good half hour. He'd never seen anyone concentrate so intensely—so intensely that he wondered if playing with the cube was doing more harm than good. After all, he had bought it for her amusement.

He turned the page, not even seeing the print. "Did I finally buy a puzzle that you can't solve?"

She glanced up at him and frowned over the cube. "This is a cruel joke, right? You've taken this thing apart and put it back together again so it can't be fixed, haven't you?"

He grinned at her. "Admit it. You're stumped."

"I'm not stumped. I'm bored with it." She tossed

the cube on the table amid piles of newspapers. "And I can't believe how easily you sucker me into playing with those toys."

"It's Sunday." *The one whole day a week I truly have alone with you.* "You're hung over from last night's bash, remember? That's the official story. You're entitled to fiddle with puzzles."

She rolled her eyes. "The rats are going to think I've turned into a hopeless lush."

Garrick would rather they knew the truth, but he knew better than to say that to Amanda. For two weeks they'd managed to keep their heated affair secret from the world, but he was beginning to hate the tangle of lies and half-truths he had to weave whenever Amanda was "late" for work. It grated on his nerves not to be able to stand on a mountaintop and scream to the whole world that *he*—and no other man—had the privilege of kissing and touching and making love to Amanda Karlson. He always wanted her most when she was least accessible—like when he stood next to her at a social event, listening to her espouse on something about wine-making, her voice even, her face immobile—and only he knew the passion beneath.

His gaze slipped over her as she reached for the muffin and took another bite. She wore those shameless cut-offs, and her long, long legs were smooth and slightly tanned. He loved those shorts. He especially loved her *out* of those shorts.

She slapped her hands together to get rid of the crumbs. "I ought to be getting to work, Garrick—"

"Stay and play table hockey with me."

"I can't."

He lowered the paper. "You told me the cabernet

grapes won't be ready for harvest for two or more weeks."

"The cellar needs to be cleaned anyway." She perched her curvy little bottom on the edge of the table. "Have you forgotten so soon that the grand opening of the Cedar Ridge Winery is next Friday?"

How could he forget? Shelley Weintraub had phoned incessantly, bothering him with details about the celebration. And the entire Kane clan was scheduled to descend upon Napa like a swarm of bees at the end of the week; he'd been making arrangements for days. Soon this rare privacy with Amanda would be suspended, until everyone cleared out and the winery went back to normal again—as normal as normal could be, when a man was having a wild, illicit affair with his loveliest, most secretive employee.

Then he remembered something else: Amanda had told him she was going to ask her sister Rachel to come to the opening if Rachel was still living in San Francisco. "Did you manage to contact your sister this week?"

"She can't come." Amanda finished her coffee and put the cup back on the table. "She's got a job in Milan. She gave up her apartment in San Francisco a couple of weeks ago. I don't know why I got my hopes up. That sister of mine lives like a gypsy, never settling down in one place, switching jobs like she's changing clothes." Amanda's eyes narrowed on Garrick. "Maybe it's best she's not coming. One look at you and she'd be hooked. She falls in and out of love at the drop of a hat."

Garrick tried to hide his interest. A woman who was afraid to love, and a woman who couldn't stop loving— both in one family. He wondered if Amanda knew how much of her own self she revealed to him by simply talking about her family.

"I don't like that look at all." She tilted her head. "What's going on in that mind of yours?"

He tossed the paper on the desk and grasped her by the waist, pulling her down toward him. "I'm thinking that it's good to know there's a younger Karlson model out there somewhere—for when this one wears out."

She gasped and batted at him playfully, not really resisting as he tumbled her onto his lap. He thrust his hand up, beneath the frayed edge of her cut-offs, and grasped one firm, rounded buttock. She made a throaty noise and arched against him. Through the soft cotton of her T-shirt, he lightly nipped the engorged peak of her breast with his teeth.

"Garrick . . ." She slipped her fingers beneath the black spandex strap and pulled it over his shoulder. "Do you wear this thing just to drive me into a frenzy?"

"Um-huh." He had discovered how much she liked this black bodysuit one morning, when he returned from rock-climbing. She had attacked him with particular vigor right here on the kitchen floor.

He unsnapped her shorts and drew the zipper down. "Don't you wear these for the same reason?"

He arched his neck and found her lips as he slowly tugged the cut-offs over her hips and down the length of her thighs. He kissed her hungrily, coaxing her passion, kissing her until her eyes grew soft and heavy-lidded, until he felt her wordless surrender. He loved that feeling most—the soft noises that escaped her throat, the heaviness of her arms, the yielding in her body. He liked to think that only he knew what raw, primitive, uninhibited passion lay beneath the cool veneer—only he could melt her.

He tugged off her cotton panties. "Isn't this better than working, Amanda?"

She nodded mindlessly, her fingernails scraping his shoulders and back. He tossed the panties to the floor. She was ready for him. The knowledge made the blood surge to his loins. His hunger for her was incessant, sharp, and the more he made love to her, the more he wanted to make love to her. He also wanted to take her out to dinner and a movie, or take her to Monterey Bay for a romantic weekend, or take her ballooning over the valley—but all those public shows of affection were forbidden. The only way he could show the strength of his feelings was by giving her presents, by playing games with her, and by making love to her as often and as passionately as possible.

He stood up, bringing her with him, laying her back on the length of the kitchen table, her now-empty cup of coffee tumbling off the edge to the floor. He finished the job she had begun stripping the spandex off his body, then pushed up her T-shirt to expose her breasts, cupped in lace. He nipped at the tight nipples, drawing them between his lips until they jutted sharply against the restriction of her bra. Then he delved his tongue into the indentation of her navel, then lower, to seek her most sensitive spot amid the dark-gold curls.

He loved touching her like this, feeling her arch and twist and cry out at the pleasure, feeling the last vestiges of her control shatter under his touch. He suckled her intimately, running his hands over her lean, curvy body. When he couldn't bear being apart from her any longer, he drew her hips to the edge of the table and lifted her legs high. The dappled morning sun spilled in through the kitchen window, lighting her hair like gold. She opened for him, and slowly he merged their bodies into one. Her muscles spasmed around him, hot and moist, and drew him deeper. Then he gripped her slim hips and loved her the only way he could—the only way she would allow him to love her.

And he did love her—as he had never loved any woman. He couldn't remember exactly when he discovered his feelings, he only knew that one day he had woken up beside her and watched her sleeping, and knew, somewhere deep inside, that she belonged by his side. So many times he had been on the brink of telling her, only to stop himself—afraid that Amanda, with all her fierce independence, with her deep-seated need to control every detail of her own life, would run far, far away if she knew the true depth of his feelings.

So he expressed his love for her the only way he could, trying to prove with every caress, with every swift, hungry kiss, that he could be trusted; that she had nothing to fear by depending upon him; that they could be lovers and friends and she could still be an individual, autonomous and strong; that loving him did not mean losing herself, or any of the independence and self-sufficiency she had battled so many years to obtain—and most of all, that it didn't mean pain.

He was winning—he knew he was. Every time they made love she gave a little more of herself. Even now, as she arched her back against the table and squeezed her eyes shut, her face flushing as she reached her climax, he felt a sense of victory.

Moments later, she lay on the table, her lips swollen from kisses, her T-shirt wrinkled up around her midriff, her ribs expanding and deflating with each deep breath. He reached under her hips, then around her shoulders, carefully drew her up, with whatever paper and debris still stuck to her back. While they were still joined, he sat down on a kitchen chair, with Amanda astride him.

He buried his face in her neck, damp from their lovemaking. Her hair formed a pale, moonlit curtain around their faces. He felt her heart pounding wildly in her chest. He still throbbed in her, deep and warm.

She glanced ruefully at the open window behind her. "Thank God the grape pickers aren't hanging around anymore."

He tightened his grip on her hips, so she wouldn't go, so she wouldn't separate their bodies—not yet.

She smiled down at him, her eyes sultry and confident. "You don't seem to mind that we just made love all over the Sunday paper."

He shrugged and kissed a pulse in her throat. "I can think of no better use for the business section."

"Is that the section stuck all over my back?"

He reached up and felt something crinkly clinging to her skin. He pulled it away and realized it was the center page of the *Napa Weekly*.

"It's just this rag." He showed it to her. "It's never been put to better use."

He was about to toss it away, but Amanda suddenly seized his arm. "Wait. Let me see that."

He held the paper up. She reached for it, straightening it so that she could see it better. Her entire body stiffened. "Oh, God. Look."

Garrick glanced at the paper. In the two right-hand columns, under Sadie Cello's heading, was a picture of him and Amanda dancing. His hand was curled tight around Amanda's waist. Her slim, reedy body was pressed flush up against him. They were looking at each other, oblivious to the camera. Oblivious, it seemed, to anyone or anything around them.

"It's not a bad picture," he said guardedly, watching Amanda's face pale. "It must have been taken at that Chenin Blanc festival over in St. Helena."

"Oh, God. . . ." Amanda struggled off him. Heedless of her semi-nudity, she yanked the paper from Garrick's grip and leaned against the table, frantically reading the column. When she finished, she crumpled the paper in one hand and covered her mouth. She stared at him with wide eyes. "It's finally happened."

"What?"

"I knew it would happen someday." She tossed the paper at him and searched the linoleum for her white cotton panties. "Oh, God, oh, God—"

Garrick uncrinkled the paper as she hopped into her cut-offs. He smoothed it over the table and read the beginning of Sadie Cello's column, right under the picture.

HAS THE ICE QUEEN MELTETH?

Another day, another bit of gossip, my curious little friends! At a recent posh Napa soiree, this little birdie witnessed Garrick Kane, well-established playboy and the owner of the Cedar Ridge Winery, wielding his notorious charm on his own lovely winemaster Amanda Karlson—and Miss Karlson drinking it in like the newest vintage. No official word, of course—but, dear reader, I say where there's smoke like that there's definitely fire!

He looked up at her. Her face flushed and she struggled to zip and snap up her cut-offs. He reached for her, but she whirled away, pacing.

She ran her hand through her tangled hair. "I was such a fool—thinking we could keep this all a secret. Sadie Cello just bathed me in muck—"

"Sadie doesn't say anything." Garrick reached for her, finally managing to capture her arm. He drew her toward him. "It's just a rumor, Amanda."

"Yes, a rumor. There's *nothing* more poisonous than a rumor to a woman's career—except maybe the truth." She glanced at him, naked on the chair, his spandex bodysuit lying discarded on the floor. She squeezed her eyes shut, then rubbed her forehead with her fingers. "Do you realize what's going to happen, Garrick, what is happening right now? Everyone in Napa is reading the column and discussing us over their scrambled eggs and bacon, remembering a dozen little incidents, speculating, wondering, imagining—"

He shrugged. "They probably are."

Her eyes flashed open and she jerked at her arm. "You don't care, do you? You've just made another *conquest*, another notch in your bedpost—"

"You're one hell of a trophy, Amanda." He yanked her closer, then pulled her forcefully onto his naked lap, trying to stop her squirming. "Today, every man in Napa is wondering how I managed to win over Amanda Karlson."

"You can tell them at the next social event." She pressed her fists against his chest, resisting all his attempts to hold her. "They're all going to pat you on the back like the hunter who brought me down, and they'll look at me as if it's open season and I'm a ten-point stag."

"Let them eat their hearts out."

"Stop it, stop it! This isn't funny. This isn't something to joke about. I'll never find another job in this valley."

Growling, he took her wrists and forcefully drew them around his neck. "Planning on quitting, Karlson?"

"Of course not—"

"Good. You don't think this will blow over in the next three, four, five years?"

She blinked. "You intend to keep me that long?"

"Amanda darling, I intend to keep you a hell of a lot longer than that."

It was the closest he had ever come to admitting he loved her. He tensed, waiting for the fear to flash in her eyes, waiting for her to jump up out of his arms and go off to work. He started to make some lighthearted, teasing reference to how long it takes to age a winemaker, but he swallowed the words, for she didn't stiffen in his embrace. Instead, the tenseness melted from her body and the anger seeped out of her eyes, leaving only a lingering tinge of uncertainty.

Progress, he thought. Progress.

"You know they'll make this seem cheap. Tawdry." She sighed and lay her head against his shoulder. "They'll wonder how I got this job. They'll think I—"

"Stop." He brushed his hands over her hair, trying to soothe her, knowing all the while that she was right. He glanced at the page, lying open and crinkled on the table. That picture condemned them far more than any of Sadie Cello's insinuations. They looked like two people deeply in love, two people so engrossed in each other that they hadn't noticed a flashbulb go off only feet away. He thought they had been so careful. Lord knows he had tried. Now men would come up to him, with a speculative gleam in their eyes, and ask questions about Amanda—questions that had nothing to do with winemaking. Amanda would have to fight off advances, fight to regain respect—all over again. The bile rose to his throat. "I won't let them hurt you."

Her fingers curled into fists against his chest. "I knew the risk when I chose to get involved with you. Now I'll have to pay the consequences."

"Like hell." He ran his fingers through her hair, brushing the pale locks away from her face. "The next event on the hyperactive Napa social calendar is the opening of this winery. That'll be our night, Amanda, and we'll prove to the whole valley that we're far above Sadie Cello's gossip."

"They'll watch us like hawks."

"Let them. We won't give them any reason to suspect there's anything more between us than friendship." He tilted her chin up, then brushed her lips. "Even if it is a bald-faced lie."

She didn't smile. She lay in his arms, silent. He knew she wasn't convinced. He knew, too, that she would bear the brunt of the destructive force of the rumor. He drew her legs higher on his, wrapped her more tightly in his embrace, wishing he could squeeze out all her doubts and fears—wishing he could make it all better.

He knew exactly how he could make it better. The idea had been hovering in the back of his mind for days. He had planned to wait—he had planned a slow and subtle attack of Amanda's defenses so that she wouldn't become frightened and take flight. Now he knew that his plans would have to be accelerated. He had to convince Amanda that love didn't always mean pain and that the rewards far outweighed the risks.

"Trust me, Amanda."

He had taken risks before; hell, he had made his fortune taking risks. But never, ever had the stakes been as high as this.

If he failed this time, he would lose Amanda.

NINE

Amanda pulled open the front door and posed in the door frame waiting for Maggie's reaction, but all of Maggie's attention was focused on the black stretch limousine parked in front of the condominium. Amanda shifted her weight, hoping the gleam of the late-afternoon sun on her dress or the sound of all those sequins scraping against each other would gain her friend's attention.

Maggie didn't even turn around. "Don't tell me Garrick sent us that, too?"

"He sure did." Amanda noticed with dark delight that the tuxedo-clad chauffeur leaning against the door gaped at her, losing his cigarette in the process. "After wangling those appointments at Luigi's Salon, he didn't want us arriving at the Cedar Ridge Opening in my pickup or your psychedelic Bug."

"My, my." Maggie patted her chestnut-colored curls, which had been effectively subdued into a frothy confection atop her head. "First he manages to get you, the worst control freak I know, off the winery, then he manages two appointments at the poshest salon in Napa, and now this.'' Maggie turned, the shocking-green skirts of her chiffon dress swinging around her legs. "I'd say you caught yourself a live one— *Amanda*!''

Amanda leaned seductively against the door frame, à la Mae West. "So, do you like it?''

Maggie's bright pink lips rounded into an O. She blinked, as if she were blinded by the rows and rows of candy-apple red sequins shimmering in the sun. "Amanda Karlson!'' She grasped her gold purse to her chest and clutched the matching gold belt that cinched in her waist. "You told me you were going to wear a 'little red dress,' but I had no idea . . .''

"Appropriate, huh?'' Defiantly, Amanda thrust a silk-stockinged knee out of the slit that ran halfway up her thigh. "I figured that since Sadie Cello painted me as a scarlet lady, I might as well look the part.''

"Battle colors.''

Amanda opened the door wider. "Come in so I can finish putting on the war paint.''

"Oooh, boy,'' Maggie said, walking into the apartment. "I don't think Sadie knows what she's in for.''

"A confusing night, that's what.'' Amanda strode to her bedroom, Maggie in tow, the high heels of her red satin shoes digging deep into the carpet. "When this night is over, not a soul in Napa is going to believe that there's anything between me and Garrick but a professional relationship.''

"Amanda, who are you kidding?'' Maggie plopped down on the queen-size bed, her chiffon skirts floating around her. She looked pointedly at Amanda's dress, sleeveless, which hugged her breasts and thrust them up high on her chest. "Garrick's only human—and he's going to have a coronary when he sees you in that."

"Hopefully," Amanda said as she leaned over her dressing table and screwed open a silver tube of lipstick, "so will every other man in Napa." She traced her lips with the vivid red color. "I plan to spend the whole night fighting them all off."

In the mirror, Amanda saw Maggie smile. "Clever, very clever. The tactics of confusion."

"If I have to, I'm going to dance with every single man attending this fête—including Mr. Garrick Kane— and I'm going to bore them with shop talk all night, too." Amanda straightened, tossed the closed lipstick into her matching red sequined purse, and snapped it shut. "Sadie Cello will burn out her overinquisitive little mind to try to sort out my love life. When she realizes she can't, she'll move on to smaller and meaner things."

Amanda curled her fingers around the open bottle of Cabernet on her dresser and filled two crystal goblets with the wine. All week she had fretted and worried over the upcoming opening, burying herself in the cellar, cleaning, fixing, shining, making everything picture perfect for the industry experts who would be wandering through the winery on the night of the opening. She tried not to think about Sadie Cello's column, but she couldn't ignore the looks she got whenever she ran errands in downtown Napa. She wondered if she'd have to face the same looks all night long at the opening. She wondered if she'd end up talking to a crowd full of lustful leers.

The night had filled her with utter dread. She had to admit Garrick had been the soul of caring, but none of his assurances really helped, as dear as he was for trying to ease her mind. There was nothing Garrick could do. She had to somehow extricate herself from the pickle she had gotten herself into. It wasn't until yesterday, when Amanda had purchased this shameless dress in a little boutique in San Francisco, when she truly began to think she could seize control of the situation.

Dad would have said it best: The best defense is a strong offense. It was time to attack.

"This is one of the first bottles of the new Cedar Ridge Cabernet to be opened." Amanda turned and handed Maggie a glass of the ruby-colored wine. "I snuck it out for a little pre-opening fortification."

"Rah, rah." Maggie stood up and raised her glass. "I propose a toast. To a successful opening, and a successful squelching of the Garrick Kane-Amanda Karlson rumor."

"Hear, hear."

Maggie took a sip of the wine, rolled it around her mouth, swallowed it, then sighed in surprise. She held the glass up to the light and swirled it, awestruck. "This is great!"

"I wish I could take credit." Amanda took another sip, and let the full black cherry taste of the wine linger on her tongue before swallowing it. "All I did was bottle the stuff. It was Mr. Brunichelli's last batch. Now Garrick owns it, since he bought the winery lock, stock, and barrel. I don't think he realizes what a gem it is."

"Well, this ought to cause a sensation tonight, but I'm afraid it won't be nearly as potent as that red flag you're waving." Maggie took another sip, hugged her arms, and swirled in the room. "I still can't believe that I—a member of the Great Unwashed—am not only going to a winery opening, but I'm actually going to watch gossip in the making!''

Amanda grunted. ''Comes with having friends in high places.''

''Well, Garrick is a sweetie for inviting me. After all, he must have known I didn't like him at first. How could I, after reading that ugly article all those weeks ago?'' She buried her nose in the wineglass and took a deep breath. ''But when he called me today, asking me to drag you away from the winery, I remembered the way he looked at you—''

''You're easy, Maggie.'' Amanda took a deep sip of the wine, trying not to think about how she and Garrick looked at each other, about how every time she met his gaze her heart leapt to her throat. ''You just like him because he got you an appointment at Luigi's.''

''Come on, you know it takes more than a facial and a manicure to win me over.'' Maggie waved the folds of her chiffon skirts. ''He's got a heart of gold to let you do this tonight.''

Amanda's gaze faltered. She turned around and placed her wineglass on the dresser.

Maggie drew in a deep breath. ''Amanda Stephanie Karlson—''

''I just haven't had time to tell him,'' she said, smoothing her hands over her hips, feeling the bite of the sequins against her palms. ''He'll understand. It's just that I only thought of this yesterday.''

''Hmm, I wonder what headline Sadie will use,'' Maggie murmured. '' 'Winery Owner Wins Wicked Winemaker'; 'Stockbroker Sleeps with Slut in Scarlet—' ''

''What is that supposed to mean?''

''It means we'd better be going.'' She placed her

glass beside Amanda's, then clutched her by the arm. "Come on, girl. You've got to let Garrick know what you've got brewing in that hyperactive mind of yours or else this whole thing is going to blow up in your face."

A half hour later, the limo pulled up in front of the Cedar Ridge Winery. A large red-and-green striped awning had been erected in the open space between the main house of the winery and the beginning of the vineyards. Chaos ruled beneath it. The caterers, dressed in black, dashed to and fro, setting up the buffet on a long table on one side of the open tent and covering the round tables with red and green tablecloths and gleaming silver and crystal. A few people Amanda assumed were from the PR firm raced around, barking orders, directing the florists as they wound garlands of roses about the posts of the tent, ordering the repositioning of tables. At the far end, on a raised dais, a swing band tested and adjusted their instruments.

Maggie bounded out of the limo like a puppy, ignoring the chauffeur's extended hand, trying to drink in the scene in one sweeping gaze. Amanda steeled herself, took the chauffeur's hand, and stepped out of the limo. The full-length dress slipped seductively off her legs, then swung back again as she stood in the driveway.

She saw Garrick immediately. He stood on the veranda, wearing a tuxedo very much like the one he had worn to the Duchamp gala the night they had first made love. He looked rich and confident—and breathtakingly handsome. Suddenly, she could no longer hear the squeals of horns and strings or the clatter of silver against china. At the sight of him, Amanda nearly lost all her bravado.

She had been kidding herself all along. How could she possibly ignore this man throughout the night? How could she possibly pretend that she wasn't completely, utterly, hopelessly in love with him?

But she had to—immediately—for Garrick was not alone. A crowd of people she had never seen before clustered around him. A slim, dark-haired young woman tugged on his arm and pointed at her and Maggie. Amanda stiffened. Garrick started down the steps, but his pace faltered on the last stair when he realized who she was.

Amanda followed Maggie toward the shade of the veranda, her legs as heavy as lead. Her blood rose to her cheeks, for he was staring at her unabashedly. She felt his gaze like a physical caress, slipping from the tips of her shoes, over the length of her legs, up the sleek, tight-fitting length of the dress to the bodice, then above, to her shoulders and to her hair. Suddenly, collecting himself, he descended the last stair and strode the last few feet across the yard to greet them.

"I told you you'd be waving a red flag in front of a bull." Maggie thrust her hand out at him, stopping him in his tracks, then raised her voice. "Thanks so much for inviting me, Garrick! I've been looking forward to this all month."

He shook Maggie's hand absently, but his eyes were not on her. Amanda tilted her chin, all too conscious of the curious stares coming from the veranda. "Hello, Garrick." She nodded toward the house. "I see some of the guests have already arrived."

"Guests?" He tore his gaze away from her for a moment to glance over his shoulder, but his gaze returned to her, like a compass needle forced to face north. "Those aren't guests. That's just the Kane clan." He lowered his voice. "Dear God, Amanda, what—"

"Your family! How charming." Maggie grasped Amanda's arm and headed toward the veranda. "Perhaps you ought to introduce us to them."

Before Garrick could say any more, Maggie urged Amanda up the stairs into the shade of the porch, right into the center of the crowd of strangers. Maggie began babbling about how excited she was about the opening, talking to no one in particular in her usual flighty way, stopping only when Garrick joined them and began a round of introductions.

Amanda tried to ignore the heat of Garrick's body, standing far too close to hers. She concentrated instead on his family. Garrick's father was as tall as Garrick, dark blond with a touch of gray at each temple, his deep-blue eyes searching and open. He gallantly kissed Amanda's outstretched hand. Garrick's mother, a short, round woman wearing blue satin with a roll of rich, dark hair perched high on her head, also ignored Amanda's hand and kissed her on each cheek. Then, looking pointedly at Amanda's bare left hand, she told Amanda how nice it was to have such a young, pretty woman working in the winery alongside her son.

Amanda smiled stiffly, wondering if Mrs. Kane knew *exactly* how closely they had been "working" lately. She glanced up at Garrick, but his face was immobile— only his eyes smoldered, with far too much heat.

She returned her attention to two sleek, willowy women who complimented her on her dress. Amanda was pleased to discover they were Garrick's two youngest sisters. His other sister waved up at Amanda while wiping dirt off her youngest boy's tiny tuxedo, while her husband, Garrick's brother-in-law, struggled with two other children. Luke, Garrick's only other sibling, leaned against the trellis, smoking a cigarette. He nodded to her and Maggie, took another drag on his cigarette, then his eyes rested in dark speculation on Maggie.

Introductions over, they all started speaking at once. Mrs. Kane couldn't stop talking about the beauty of the valley and the mountains, about the perfect location of the winery. She asked to be shown around the cellar tomorrow, when all the fuss was over. Amanda agreed to a private tour. She was vividly conscious of Garrick beside her, joking with his father, bending to tickle one of his nephews, then teasing his sisters and Maggie as the three single women clustered to one side of the veranda to scan the waiters and the men in the band. Since she had arrived, he had not once left her side.

She felt someone plucking at her dress. She looked down and saw Garrick's youngest nephew running his hands over the rows and rows of sequins. Sensing her gaze, he looked up at her, a little star-struck by all the glitter. The boy had dark hair and blue eyes, just like Garrick. She smiled at him. She wondered if Garrick had looked this adorable when he was a child. She wondered if Garrick's son would be as adorable.

She wondered if she and Garrick would ever have a child together.

She started inwardly. Where did *that* thought come from? She and Garrick weren't even married—they hadn't even spoken of love—and children were a life-long responsibility. She had never planned to have children. She had never *wanted* to have children.

Didn't she?

Suddenly, the boy dove through the slit in her dress and wrapped himself, giggling, in the red glitter.

Amanda, knocked slightly off balance, reached out. Garrick caught her waist as she swayed toward him.

"Looks like you've got another admirer."

"Ricky!" Garrick's sister raced over and untangled the boy from her dress and legs. She swung her hair out of her eyes and looked up at Amanda. "Sorry, Amanda."

"It's okay." She straightened the dress to hide her legs, at the same time trying in vain to pull away from Garrick's embrace. "It's the sequins, that's all."

"More likely it was the treasure beneath."

Amanda jerked away from Garrick. He had whispered the words, so close that she could feel the moisture of his breath in her ear, but he knew better than to say something so seductive, even if the only people around were members of his family. She glanced at his sister, but she was too wrapped up in gently scolding her son to notice.

Amanda gathered a fistful of sequins in one hand. "I'll leave you with your family, Mr. Kane. I have some last-minute things to attend to in the cellar—"

"You're not getting away so easily, Amanda."

She lowered her voice. "Garrick, you promised—"

"I need you here." He gestured to the drive. The first car approached, the first guests of the evening. "We have to welcome our guests."

She relaxed. Of course, she must stay; of course, she must stand next to Garrick as the guests arrived. She had overreacted. Garrick released her. He herded his family and Maggie off the veranda, ordering them to mingle beneath the awning. He returned to her side just as the valet in crisp whites opened the door to the first car.

His voice was soft in her ear. "Showtime, Amanda."

She put on her social smile and welcomed the restaurateur and her husband, who had driven up from San Francisco. After a few minutes of small talk, Garrick shuttled them over to the awning and the tuxedoed man waiting with a tray full of sparkling wine. Another car arrived and she and Garrick welcomed them with the same warmth.

Ten minutes later, there was a lull in the arrivals. The hairs stood up on the back of Amanda's neck as she realized that she and Garrick were alone.

"Witch," he whispered. "Are you trying to get me arrested for carrying a lethal weapon?"

She met his hot gaze, then looked down and noticed the effect she had on him. She felt a thrill of purely feminine victory. "Do you object to my dressing for success?"

"I wouldn't, if you were dressed." He ran a hand through his hair, completely messing up the crisp waves, and glared at the shadows between her breasts. "Christ, Amanda. From this angle, I can see all the way to L.A."

"You're not supposed to be looking."

"Right. And tell Pavlov's dogs not to salivate at the sound of a bell." He shoved his fists into his pockets. "I expected you to be covered from head to toe, as demure as a virgin bride."

"I'm not giving Sadie Cello the satisfaction." She allowed her lips to curve into a slight smile as she watched the valet approach another car. "I intend to be the belle of the ball tonight and throw Sadie Cello and her ilk completely off the scent."

"More likely you'll start a feeding frenzy." He lowered his brows. "What do you mean, 'belle of the ball?' "

She shrugged, then painted on her rigid smile as the valet opened the car door. "I'm going to dance with a few people. More than usual. All the young, single men. Just long enough to confuse the hell out of Sadie Cello."

His voice came out raw and rough. "What makes you think I'll let any other men near you?"

"You don't have a choice." She straightened her back, keeping the stiff smile on her face, trying to stifle her involuntary reaction to the raw possessiveness in his voice. "Keep your eyes and your hands off me tonight—or I'll never forgive you, Kane, for as long as you live." She held out her hand as the new arrival approached. "Mr. Marshall, I'm so glad you could come . . ."

Mr. Marshall and two of his associates lingered longer than usual, until Garrick finally managed to shuttle them off toward the awning.

"Marshall couldn't drag his eyes above breast level."

"Garrick, he's about five feet four. He didn't have a choice."

"I don't give a damn." He tugged on the edges of his tuxedo jacket. "Hell, I wish you had just trusted me instead of coming here dressed like a femme fatale."

"I *am* trusting you. I'm trusting you to keep your eyes to yourself—"

"You should have worn a potato sack."

"This is my reputation on the line." She spoke through her teeth as another car drove up. "I'm using all the tools at my disposal to save it."

"You forget that I'm the only one allowed to play with those tools." He leaned closer, his breath brushing her ear. "When this damned opening is all over, I'm going to strip that dress off your body with my teeth."

Amanda started and suddenly lost control of her breath. She coughed, hoping to hide her reaction from the next set of guests. Damn Garrick Kane. Damn him for feeding her some of her own medicine.

When she finally straightened and apologized, she knew the tips of her ears had grown as red as her dress. But there was no more time for whispered communication. The guests arrived one after another, the cars lined up clear down the road. She and Garrick spent a good forty-five minutes welcoming each and every one of them. Amanda saw the open speculation on some of their faces as they looked from her to Garrick, but she maintained her stiff smile and spoke the pat phrases required of her and then shuffled them over in favor of the next group. Sadie Cello arrived, in a blinding, flowery dress, her eyes all atwinkle. Amanda congratulated herself for simply shaking her hand and welcoming her—and not cutting the witch down at the knees. Garrick, despite his earlier heated words, was the soul of discretion.

She knew that simply their presence together at the front of the winery was dulling the edge of the rumor. If Garrick had welcomed the guests alone, there would have been speculation. But right now, she and Garrick seemed like business partners, welcoming potential business clients, trying to throw one hell of a bash and get the name of the Cedar Ridge Winery on the map— immune to the scandal that was supposed to be swirling around them.

But standing next to him, Amanda felt like more than a partner, far more than a mistress. Suddenly, she realized she felt very much like a wife.

She shook her head free of the foolish thoughts. She was *not* his wife—and there was no indication that she would ever be Garrick's wife. There hadn't even been words of love between them, though she sensed that he felt more for her than simple friendship, more than lust. It was too soon for her to be wishing for such things. They had only known each other a few brief, crazy months, but it was enough time to change her world. She had grown to need him, like she never thought she'd ever need anyone. Moreover, she had grown to want the comfort and the safety she felt whenever she was in his arms.

Saftey . . . She once believed that there could be no safety in love. These past weeks she had been thinking a lot, of the time before Dad's death, when their family was whole. She found herself remembering when she was a little girl and she and her sisters would climb into bed with her parents on Sunday mornings and play hide-and-seek under the flannel sheets. She was beginning to wonder—she *dared* to wonder—if the fifteen years Mom and Dad and she and her sisters had shared—those glorious, sunny years before Dad died— could possibly be worth all the pain and struggle that followed.

Garrick was making her think crazy things—like perhaps love didn't always bring pain . . . and if it did, perhaps the love alone was worth the risk.

The sun slipped behind the ridge of the valley by the time she and Garrick welcomed the last guests. Shelley Weintraub, who Garrick introduced as the head PR person, fluttered over and urged them to join the party. Amanda dropped her purse at the head table and left Garrick to work the east side of the opening while she worked her way west. Yellowish lanterns hanging from the scaffolding of the awning cast a friendly, golden glow over the gathered guests. She was pleased—all the right people had come. She was still aware of lots of speculative looks, and Sadie Cello's eyes were on her like beacons. Determined to squash the talk once and for all, she straightened her spine and sought out the most handsome men in the room—and the most important—on whom to focus her undivided attention. Temporarily.

Soon, the buffet was opened and the guests settled down to dinner. She worked her way back to the head table, stopping at the buffet first to fill a plate with baby asparagus in a lemony hollandaise sauce, spicy wild rice, and slivers of roast duck—the perfect complement to the robust Cedar Ridge Cabernet being served with dinner.

Amanda found a seat at the head table, near Garrick's sister, brother-in-law, nieces and nephews. Luke and Maggie joined her soon after. As she took her first bite of the fresh young asparagus, Garrick sat down beside her. She glanced at the crowd beneath the veil of her lashes, wondering if it was a good idea for her and Garrick to eat together.

He pulled his chair in decisively. "How's the battle going?"

She took a sip of the wine, refusing to look at him, sensing that if she looked into his eyes, the world would be able to see her heart. "The Cabernet's a hit. I've already got two orders. I just wish we had more of it."

"They'll be begging for it in a couple of years, when this year's harvest is ready for bottling." He dug into his heaping plate of food. "But that isn't the battle that I was talking about."

"No casualties yet in the other war." She toyed with her food. "Apart from a few sly looks, Sadie Cello's incessant stare, a couple of twitters, it hasn't been all that bad."

"Lucky you." He took a sip of his wine and suppressed a grimace. "I've wanted to strangle a couple of young pups already for making comments about the lovely hills of Cedar Ridge."

"That's what you get for being such a successful hunter, Kane."

When coffee was served, the band started playing. Couples drifted onto the dance floor. Garrick excused himself to tug his mother to her feet. Amanda knew it was time to work the room again, though her throat was becoming sore from talking, her face stiff from smiling and laughing. She put her napkin aside and wandered through the tables.

Finally, finding herself at the edge of the tent, she decided to slip away from the party for a moment. She needed to get away from everything, to breathe freely without worrying that some photographer would catch her off guard staring wistfully in Garrick's direction. She took a deep breath of the fresh mountain air as she headed toward the veranda. A number of people lingered in the yard, staring up at the stars in the clear sky, watching the first fingers of fog seep over the ridge. She nodded as she passed them and entered the winery.

As usual, there was a line for the bathroom. Rather than stopping to wait, she bypassed the line and headed down the hall, deciding to pass through the main house and see if the line for the facilities in the wine cellar was as long. As she neared the kitchen, she stopped at the sound of her name. Someone was talking about her. She recognized one voice as belonging to Shelley Weintraub, the head of the PR firm in San Francisco. The other woman's voice was unfamiliar.

"She's head winemaker of Cedar Ridge." Shelley Weintraub made a noise as if she were blowing smoke through her lips. "Makes you sick, doesn't it?"

The other woman clicked her tongue. "She looks like she just stepped off the cover of *Vogue*."

"Women who can wear dresses like that should be shot."

"Now, now, Shelley, there's no reason to be jealous—"

"According to the papers, there is." Shelley lowered her voice. "Apparently she and Garrick have been making more than wine these past weeks."

"You're kidding!"

"Nope. The *Napa Weekly* ran an article under the gossip column, with an utterly incriminating picture." Shelley laughed, a deep, humorless laugh. "He's done it before, you know, had his name linked in the papers with some woman just to generate publicity for his investment firm."

"Yeah, but his own employee?"

"All the better—more scandal, more publicity."

"And there's no such thing as bad publicity."

The two women said the phrase together and laughed. Amanda's stomach turned. How quickly a rumor turned ugly. She straightened her shoulders, prepared to round the corner and enter the kitchen and let these women know *exactly* what she thought of them— but she stopped herself; she knew that would only add fuel to the fire.

"Kane's been pulling the wool over our eyes all these months," Shelley continued. "For all his absentmindedness, he's turning out to be a brilliant strategist."

"I still don't believe she's a winemaker. Winemakers

don't wear sequins—they hide in labs and don't sleep with their bosses."

"Can you blame the woman? Garrick's the hottest thing I've seen in years. And rich, to boot." Shelley lowered her voice. "And I happen to know that she *is* a winemaker. I checked. She was one of the women on the list we gave him when he first talked about hiring one."

"Is she any good?"

"Who cares? All that matters is that she fits the image the firm wanted for Cedar Ridge." Shelley stubbed out the cigarette. "We told Garrick to hire the sexiest winemaker in Napa. I just never expected him to take us quite so *literally*."

TEN

Shelley's words echoed discordantly in Amanda's ears. Blindly, she whirled and stumbled down the hall past the line of women waiting to use the bathroom and burst out into the cool freshness of the night air.

A handful of people stood on the stairs of the veranda, puffing blue streams of cigarette smoke toward the star-studded sky. The guests stared at her, mute. Realizing in some dim corner of her mind that she must look half-crazed, she smiled inanely and made a comment about the weather, then excused herself, straightened her back, and walked around the veranda to the back of the house.

Out of sight of the guests, she slumped against the trellis. She pressed her forehead against the rough bark of a woody wisteria vine and squeezed her eyes shut. It couldn't be true—it couldn't be true. She tried to convince herself she had misheard, but the words echoed back to her, as clear and crisp as the mountain air. She tried to convince herself it was just a vicious insinuation from a jealous woman, but Amanda knew that, too, wasn't true. Shelley Weintraub controlled the Cedar Ridge account, Shelley was the PR woman Garrick had been talking to on the phone all these past weeks, Shelley would know the truth—for Shelley would have been the one to give the advice.

She squeezed her eyes tighter. Suspicions she had long put aside returned to the fore. The first day she had met him, she had suspected there was some other reason Garrick chose to hire her, when a hundred other winemakers of greater reputation would have leapt at the chance to head Cedar Ridge. *This* reason made sense—horrifying, ugly sense. Image was everything in this dirty business, and what more marketable package could Cedar Ridge display than a sexy female winemaker with a playboy owner at the helm?

Oh, God. . . . Amanda slid down one of the poles of the veranda, the sequins of her dress catching on the wood. His words floated back to her, the words he had spoken the first day he hired her. *There's another reason why I want to hire you, Amanda.* Her stomach made a sickening lurch. *You're a woman.* He had told her . . . *he had told her.* What a fool she had been all this time. Her conceit alone made her think he had hired her for her expertise, that he respected her talents as a winemaker. In truth, he hadn't looked beyond her face, her breasts, her legs . . . just like a thousand other men.

She shook her head sharply. This was Garrick, *Garrick.* The man who took her up on the ridge and insisted she teach him how to tell a good wine from a bad one. The man who had deferred to her judgment in all decisions concerning the cellar. The man who had played table hockey with her until she forgot about her work, until she forgot about everything. The man who had seduced her into loving him . . . long after he knew how frightened she was to love.

She struggled to understand. Perhaps Garrick had grown to respect her work. Somehow, the thought only hurt all the more. Garrick was one of the few men with whom she had never had to pretend—the first man who had accepted her as intelligent from the moment they met. Or so she thought. Now she wasn't so sure—she wasn't sure of anything. He had hired her because she was a woman. The sexiest winemaker in Napa.

She had blinded herself to the truth.

The shark of Wall Street hadn't perished with Dominick after all. How cool-headed a decision he had made; how shrewd and heartless. An ugly thought flickered through her mind: Their relationship had created more than a little sensationalism—it had gotten his and Cedar Ridge's name in the papers.

There's no such thing as bad publicity.

She covered her eyes with her hand. She was thirty years old, not some naive little girl. She had thought Garrick felt something for her. Could she really have been so deftly fooled, so cleverly maneuvered? Could Garrick really be so ruthless to toy with her affections so lightly, to risk her career, and her heart, when he knew how hard she had protected both? There hadn't been words of love between them—and now she began to wonder if she had been imagining all those soft, loving looks in Garrick's eyes.

"Miss Karlson?"

Amanda started and looked up. A young man in a black tuxedo climbed the back stairs to the veranda.

"Are you all right, Miss Karlson?"

She straightened against the post. In her self-absorption, she had forgotten that there was a party going on and she was the hostess. She ran her hands over her sequins. "Oh, yes. I'm fine. Just a little tired."

She wondered at the evenness of her voice.

"These things can be really grueling, huh?"

She smiled thinly, noticing for the first time how stiff and sore her face muscles had become from a night's worth of social smiling. Amanda recognized the young man as the son of the owner of one of the larger wineries, but for the life of her, she couldn't remember his name. It didn't matter. What *did* matter was that her behavior was odd and he knew it—and she didn't want anyone speculating as to the cause of her abrupt flight from the party—more so now than ever. "I needed to get away from the noise for a few minutes, to catch my breath."

"I know what you mean." The young man's teeth were startlingly white against his tanned skin. "Whenever my father throws a bash, he escapes into his study with a bottle of wine and a few friends right after the music starts, just to get away from all the noise."

Amanda made the necessary laugh, wondering if it sounded as false to his ears as to hers. Apparently it didn't, for he continued to talk. She smiled politely as a night breeze filtered through the leaves and tugged at the wisps which had fallen out of her sleek French braid. How easily she fell into this role of winemaster/hostess, entertaining every guest, all for the good of Cedar Ridge. How quickly she had begun to think of this winery as her own home.

Home. A place of warmth and comfort and security. The last place where she had felt this sense of belonging was at her farm in Massachusetts, before Dad died.

Somehow, the condo she had bought three years ago had never felt like home. Something had always been missing. She thought she had found that something in this little mountain valley; she thought she had found it in Garrick's embrace. For years, she had tried to live without love, afraid of depending on anyone or anything but herself—burying herself in the one thing she could control: her career. Under Garrick's spell, she finally realized that she had been running away from the one thing that could truly make her happy—and now she didn't even know if that love was real.

"Miss Karlson?"

The young man had asked her a question, and for the life of her, she didn't know what it was. "You'll have to excuse me." She brushed past him to head around the veranda. "I'm afraid I've been neglecting my duties for too long—"

"Well, maybe we can dance later."

She paused. A rogue lock of pale blond hair fell over his forehead as he glanced down at the floorboards. She suddenly realized that he was shy—that he probably was blushing, though she couldn't tell in the dark—that he really was little more than a college boy.

She peered at him more intently. He was a *handsome* young man, for all his shy youth. She had intended to spend the night battling Sadie Cello's ugly rumors, and with the recent revelations, that battle was more important than ever. There was no reason why this young man couldn't be her first conquest of the evening.

"Let's dance now." She walked to his side and linked her arm through his. "After all, a hostess should enjoy her own party, shouldn't she?"

An hour later, Amanda was still dancing, this time with a distributor who had obviously left his wife at home, and who, by the redness of his cheeks, had imbibed too much of the Cedar Ridge Cabernet. Amanda wore a rigid smile while she whirled around the floor, laughing thinly when he made a feeble attempt at a joke, pausing to pose for the photographers who lingered. As the flash went off in her face, she ticked off the number five in her mind—for now five pictures of her had been taken dancing with men other than Garrick Kane.

Garrick, she avoided. Whenever she saw him out of the corner of her eye, hovering, watching her, she would find an excuse to walk in the opposite direction, or she would demand a dance from a passing male. Her composure hung on ragged threads, and she knew if she faced him now all her false gaiety would melt away and her heart would lie raw and open for all to see. She didn't need the press capturing the moment of her defeat on film. She needed to keep up the pace, to laugh over the pain, to smile and flirt until the tail lights of the last car disappeared down the road—then, and only then, could she turn to Garrick and show him the face of her anger.

So she danced. The music and voices, the scent of heavy perfume and sweat, all filled her head. As the dance ended, the distributor led her off to the side, mopping his brow with a handkerchief he had pulled out of his jacket. He told her he'd be right back and headed toward the main building. She took a glass of champagne from a passing waiter and sipped the potent brew, hardly feeling the tiny bite of the tingling liquid as it slid down her throat. She hardly felt real. She hardly felt human. The real Amanda Karlson floated somewhere above all the gaiety, throbbing in pain.

"You can't dodge me this time, Amanda. We've got business to take care of."

Garrick loomed in front of her. She stared at him, wondering if he would disappear as suddenly as he appeared, if she had just conjured him up out of her thoughts. But he didn't. He stayed. Her brittle patina of merriment crumbled and her falsely buoyed spirits fell to earth with a painful thud.

Damn him for being so handsome.

His eyes changed, softened. "What's wrong?"

Wrong? The whole world was wrong. Everything she had come to believe had been proven false, and now she didn't even know if she looked into the eyes of a lover or a snake. Her fingers tightened around the delicate stem of the champagne glass. Words surged to her throat, accusing words, angry, hateful words. She bit her lower lip to stop them. If she spoke them now, the floodgates would burst open and she would rage—and make a scene worse than any found in a daytime soap opera. So she finished her champagne, not tasting it as it slid down her throat, and forced her voice to function. "Let's go, Garrick. Business always comes first."

She felt his sharp scrutiny on her face, but people surrounded them, chattering, watching, forcing his attention away from her so that he could question her no more. He shouldered a path through the crowds to the dais. He spoke briefly to the leader of the band, and the music stopped. She noticed tiny, inconsequential things as Garrick drew her onto the platform; she smelled the faint scent of burnt rubber, as if some tiny piece of the band's equipment had short-circuited. She heard a glass fall and shatter somewhere on the dance floor. Garrick's hand felt cold and damp.

She glanced over the heads of the crowd, blinded by

the footlights. Her mouth felt as if it were wired open. Garrick had the microphone in his hand and was saying something, she didn't really know what—something about his arrival at the winery; something about commitment to excellence, something about a partnership. She tuned it out, knowing that it was the usual "we-stand-for-quality" speech that every winery owner gave at his annual bash. She wondered if he would ask her to say anything; she wondered if she were capable of anything other than a primordial scream.

The sound of two hundred and fifty individual gasps brought her attention back to the moment. Garrick was watching her intently—the entire party had grown so still and quiet that she could hear the shimmer of a breeze wafting over the vineyard.

She had missed her cue; she looked at him for help. Garrick took her hand and drew her close. Dangerously close. The press was watching; she straightened her back but did not pull away.

"The opening of this winery is more than just a start at a new career." Garrick slipped an arm around her shoulders. "It's a start of a new life. For both of us."

Flashbulbs exploded in her eyes as his words exploded in her head.

"This night, my friends . . . Amanda Karlson has consented to be my wife."

Garrick had to tip his hat to Amanda; the lady was cool under pressure. But for a sudden heaviness of her body—quickly corrected—she acted as if his proposal, or, rather, his declaration, had been fully planned. She smiled brightly; she accepted the applause of the crowd, she posed with him for the press. She airily brushed off any questions that delved too deeply into the details of their sudden engagement, of the coming wedding. She acted sufficiently moved through his mother's tearful welcome into the family, kissed his brother and sisters, managed to evade Maggie's pointed and suspicious surprise. Once, Amanda even gazed up at him with the expression of an adoring fiancée.

But damn it, he had envisioned the moment differently. He had hoped all that wretched Karlson composure would melt away, not harden into stone; he wanted the whole world to see the face she only showed to him. He had imagined her wrapping her arms around him, kissing him, or maybe even doing something impulsive and reckless—like dragging him off to a bedroom in front of all the gathered guests. Now he surreptitiously searched for a sign, a squeeze of her hand, a softness in her cheek, anything—*anything*— that would show him that this was what she wanted, that he wasn't risking his pride and his hopes and his future with her in vain.

He received that sign several hours later, while they bid their guests good-bye under the midnight sky. During a lull between departures, Amanda looked square at him.

Her eyes were like chips of ice.

Once, not long ago, Garrick had rented a small plane to fly him high up over some open countryside. He had strapped a parachute on his back and jumped out of the side of the plane to free-fall through the air. His ears had roared; his insides had tumbled and tightened; the wind had rushed out of his lungs. He felt the same way now, except for one small detail. Then, he had taken the risk just for the sheer thrill of it. This time, the risk was for real—and he had no parachute.

The night dragged. After most of the guests had left,

Garrick broke away from Amanda to immerse himself in other work—checking on the caterers busy taking down the tent and loading the dirty china into a van, listlessly talking to a confused and speculative Shelley Weintraub about a press release, ushering his weary, overexcited family into the house for the night. When he finally summoned the nerve to face Amanda again, she and the limo he had hired for her had disappeared into the night.

He shoved his hands into his pockets and wandered around to the side of the house, where the flattened grass gleamed in the starlight. Fog bled over the ridge, seeping down through the vineyards to pool on the valley floor. The oversweet scent of ripe fruit hung in the air. The silence of the still night was deafening after the noise of the party.

He balled his hands into fists. Standing on the edge of the vineyards, he felt like the only man in the world. He was lonely, lonelier than even in those days after Dominick's death. Amanda should be here. She belonged here, in this place, with him. Damn it, he had tried too hard; he had grasped too tightly—he had wanted her too much. Without her, this winery was nothing but a building and a plot of land—not a home.

A home. He looked up at the stars and shook his head. *Perhaps that's what I've been searching for since you've been gone, Dominick. Perhaps that's what we dreamed of all along.*

Out of the corner of his eye he saw a light flicker in the window of the wine cellar. His heart leapt. There was only one person he knew who would be banging around in that cold, musty lab at this hour of the night. He turned his footsteps toward it, his pace swift and silent over the ground.

Inside, Amanda leaned against a table, still dressed in her sheath of red sequins. She winced as she tugged a satin high-heeled pump off her foot.

He stood in the open doorway, staring at her, his heart in his throat. "I thought you had left."

"Oh?"

"Yes." He searched for words. "The limo is gone."

"I sent Maggie home in it; you and I have business to discuss." She settled her shoes on the table behind her. Her gaze could freeze fire. "Lock the door behind you, Garrick. I want no witnesses to this."

He turned his back and slid the bolt into place, struggling for some way to make this confrontation easier. "I hope," he began, as lightly as he could manage, "that you're not as skilled a taskmaster as Sister Mary O'Connell."

She blinked at him blankly.

"Sister Mary O'Connell was my second-grade teacher. She always had me lock the door before she rapped me on the wrists with her ruler." The humor fell flat; he wished he hadn't even tried. "Obviously, you didn't go to Catholic school."

"No."

The silence stretched between them. She rubbed the arches of her feet. He waited, tearing his eyes away from the sight of her long legs, his heart aching. She straightened and toyed with a piece of glassware on a nearby shelf.

"What are your plans for Cedar Ridge, Garrick?"

Her voice was soft, even, icily calm, as it had been all night. This was not what he expected. "I don't know." He paused, trying to think beyond the tension of the moment. "They haven't changed. Make the best wine possible. Sell it at an outrageous price." He managed a humorless laugh. "Do what I usually do: make lots of money."

"You're certainly off to a good start."

You, he thought. Not "we." You.

"Lots of publicity," she continued. "A nice big splash of an opening. You do have a flair for the dramatic, Kane." She folded her hands in her lap. "How long did you think I'd go along with it?"

He felt a cold draft shiver up his back. "What are you talking about?"

"The marriage thing. How long did you think I'd let you go on with it?"

His shoulders weighed a hundred thousand pounds. "I was hoping . . . forever."

She turned her back to him and pushed away from the table. She strolled toward one of the gleaming fermentation tanks. She idly rubbed a spot on the stainless steel. Her French braid, so sleek and tight earlier in the evening, had loosened and given way to wisps which lay soft and vulnerable on her shoulders and nape.

"I never liked surprises, Garrick." Her voice cracked ever so slightly, a hesitation he noticed only because he had spent weeks studying every sweet inflection of her voice. "The only thing I dislike more is lies."

"Lies?" His eyes flew to her profile. "Is that what this is, Amanda? Do you think this is all a lie?"

"I don't know what else to call it. I've never known anyone who would go so far . . . for publicity."

"Publicity?!"

"What have you got to lose?" She swung her arms wide. "If I had made a scene, the papers would have run red with the story tomorrow. If I actually held you to your promise, I'm sure you'd orchestrate a splashy break-up when the fervor from the announcement died down. Either way, the papers would be covered with the name Cedar Ridge and you'd make lots of money.''

He was too stunned to speak, too confused by the convoluted way her mind worked. She had always been overly concerned about gossip, but she couldn't be serious . . . couldn't really believe he'd ask her to marry him just to generate press. She knew him better than that. . . . It had to be something else. Perhaps this was her way of resisting him. Perhaps this was the final, brittle barrier in her armor. He fumbled in the pockets of his jacket and pulled out a small velvet box. ''Always the scientist,'' he said gruffly. ''Well, this ought to be enough proof of my good intentions, Einstein.''

Her gaze fell upon the box. He thought he saw something glimmer in her eye, but she squeezed her eyes shut, then pressed her forehead against the tank. ''My God. You even have props.''

''Props?''

''Is it at least tax-deductible, Garrick?'' Her voice broke again—harsher. ''An advertisement expense?''

''What the hell—'' He shoved the box back in his pocket and crossed the distance that separated them. He gripped her bare shoulders—hard. ''Do you think I make marriage proposals everyday, Amanda?''

He regretted the angry words as soon as he spoke them; when she looked up at him, he saw that the ice had melted into tears.

He bit off an expletive. ''Tell me what the hell is going on.''

''I overheard Shelley Weintraub,'' she began heatedly, ''exclaiming about how shrewd you were to hire me.''

''It was the best decision I ever made.''

''She agreed.'' She leveled him with her direct green

gaze. "She told you to hire the sexiest winemaker in Napa."

Amanda waited. She felt the chill of the stainless steel tank at her back. She smelled the scent of Garrick's cologne, warmed by the heat of his body. She waited for his denial, willing him wordlessly to call Shelley a bald-faced liar, but he said nothing. Something flickered in his dark blue eyes. He loosened his grip on her shoulders.

She drew in a long, agonizing breath, then covered her mouth with a trembling hand. She didn't know until now what she had expected from him. Somewhere, deep inside her, she had hoped he would give her an utter, vehement denial—she expected him to repudiate the whole idea. For if Shelley lied, for whatever reason, then maybe, just maybe, this marriage proposal was more than just a publicity stunt . . . just maybe Garrick Kane really did want to make her his wife.

Yet he stood in front of her, shame-faced, and she knew for sure that Shelley's words were true.

"Oh, my God . . ."

"Amanda, it's not as you think."

She twisted away from him. She didn't want him to see her tears, she didn't want him to see how deeply he had thrust the knife. She thought about all their lazy Sunday afternoons, all the hours of lovemaking, all the games and the laughter. Lies.

The marriage proposal, too.

Lies, lies, lies.

"Hell, Amanda, I never thought you'd find out." He stepped back and raked his fingers through his hair. "I didn't think there was any reason to tell you—"

"Of course not." She tried to make her voice frosty;

she hated herself for failing. "You knew what I would have done if I had known the truth."

"This is the truth: I hired you for your brains."

"Really?" She dug her manicured nails into her bare arms. "You wanted to hire a woman. Shelley Weintraub gave you my name. You called me, interviewed me for ten minutes, and hired me without ever speaking to anyone else—"

"Do you think I'd put the future of this winery in the hands of a bubblehead just because she had great legs?"

"No, I didn't!" She dared to glare at him, finding a thread of strength in anger. "After tonight, after that . . . *stunt* you pulled, what else am I supposed to believe?"

"A stunt? Is that really all you think it was?"

Amanda held her chin steady. Dad would be proud of her; she wouldn't let Garrick see her bleed.

"I thought you knew me better by now." He stepped back, then turned away. He wandered through the room aimlessly, then sank onto a bench, his hands clenched in his pockets. "I won't deny it—I heard of you because you were on Shelley's list and I needed someone fast and that list was as good a place to start looking as any. Miguel spoke well of you, too, which was another reason why I called. But it didn't take more than ten minutes to know you were one hell of a winemaker. You should have enough confidence in yourself to know that. Hiring you was a business decision, fair and square."

"A brilliant one, according to Shelley—"

"For God's sake, she's not a consultant, she's part of a PR firm! When she told me what she wanted, I told her to go straight to hell. All a PR firm cares about is glitter and publicity—''

"Yes, *publicity*." She swallowed the lump growing in her throat. "Like the kind you get from seducing your own employee."

His footsteps scraped on the cement floor; she was not quick enough to avoid him. His hands curled around her shoulders and he pulled her back against his chest. His voice was husky and ragged, his breath hot on her hair. "Hell, yes, I intended to seduce you from the moment I laid eyes on you—''

"You *bastard*—''

"—but I didn't plan it for the publicity, any more than I pulled tonight's 'stunt' for the publicity. Do you want to know why, Amanda? Do you want to hear everything? Hell, why not? I haven't any pride left anyway, and what good is pride when you've got nothing to be proud of?"

Amanda's anger ebbed; there was something in the timbre of his voice, something in the tense grip he had on her shoulders that told her there was more honesty to this than she had ever heard from any man, from any person.

"I wanted to seduce you for one reason only: because you were unlike any woman I've ever known—brilliant and honest and determined and principled. Because I wanted to unveil the lonely woman who hid behind all that armor, because I wanted to take you in my arms and show you all the joy in the world that you hid from in this damned laboratory."

Her breath froze in her lungs. She felt her anger crumble; she felt everything crumble around her. In his arms she was becoming weak . . . vulnerable. "Don't, Garrick—''

"It's too late. You're going to hear this and hear it through and when I'm done you can do what you want." He wound his arms around her and buried his face in the nape of her neck. "I've spent weeks trying to show you that you can depend on someone without being afraid, that there's more joy in loving someone for ten minutes than living alone and unloved for a lifetime. I thought by now you knew me well enough to trust me." His voice broke as his arms tightened around her. "Hell, I thought you might even love me. Because, Lord knows, I'm head over heels in love with you."

The words echoed in the cellar. She stiffened, not sure she had heard him right, wordlessly willing him to say them again—*say them again*. She tried to twist, but he held her too tightly, and as she jerked, his embrace tightened even more.

"Don't run away from me, Amanda."

Her heart skipped a beat; that was anxiety in his voice, untempered, bald anxiety. A tremor rippled through her—the burgeoning of hope.

"For a year and a half I've been searching for something. When Dominick died, everything I'd spent a lifetime working for seemed . . . meaningless. Money had become a goal in itself, not the comfort and ease and pleasure and good that money can buy. I've been wandering, searching. Hell, I don't know what for. Roots, maybe. A home. Something permanent." His voice deepened. "Something I found when I came here and met you."

"Why . . . why didn't you tell me all this before?"

"I intended to. Every single time we made love, every time we were alone. I was afraid you'd run away. I thought you'd fight against giving up some of that damn stubborn independence you value so much, against giving up control over your life.'' He paused, his voice growing wry. ''So I thought I'd tell you in front of two hundred and fifty people—when you couldn't say no. I knew you wouldn't make a scene.''

''Garrick . . .''

''You could leave now, Amanda. You could say no and leave.'' He dropped his arms and took one step back, not so far that she couldn't still feel the heat of his body. ''I've had my say. Hell, if you don't want me now, just go. Don't stay for pity's sake.''

The room grew quiet enough for her to hear her own breathing—and to know that he was holding his breath. She turned and looked into his eyes. ''This isn't pity, Garrick.''

She moved into his arms and felt the shock reverberate through his body. His arms closed around her. She pressed her forehead against his, and they both drew in the same, trembling breath.

Words bubbled to her throat, words she should have said long ago. Only now, in the face of Garrick's love, had she found the strength to be vulnerable.

''I don't know when it happened.'' She let the confession cleanse her of fear. ''I don't know when I finally realized how narrow and controlled my life was; I don't know when I realized that what you had been teaching me all along was how to play.'' She glanced down at the golden light glimmering off the sequins of her dress and managed a shaky laugh. ''Two months ago, I would have given up my career before I ever wore a dress like this. You do things like that to me. It's a little bit of magic, I think.'' He started to say something; she distracted him with the briefest of kisses. ''Somewhere along the way, I realized that I was in love with you." The words sprang to her lips easier than she had ever imagined they would. "That's what keeps me here; that's what has kept me here all these weeks, when I knew it would be best for my own peace of mind to run to the ends of the world. Now it's too late. I love you, Garrick. I love you—"

His lips came down upon hers, demanding, insistent. The scent of his battered rose boutonniere wafted up between them. Her heart swelled and she pressed closer, wanting nothing between them but skin and love and soft words. He loved her—*he loved her*—all that mattered was the brush of his lips against her neck, the impatience in his kiss, the love burning between them.

Garrick pulled away and fumbled in his jacket. He tossed the velvet box to the floor and slipped the ring on her finger. "I'm doing all this backwards," he said, his voice low and gravelly, "but, hell, I've always hated the direct route to the top of a cliff—and this has been one hell of a climb." He framed her face in his hands. "Marry me, Amanda. Be Mrs. Garrick Kane, or *Ms.* Amanda Karlson, wife of Garrick Kane—whoever you want to be. Just tell me you'll be my wife."

Wife. She savored the sound of the word echoing in the room. It sounded safe and permanent. Unpredictable. Glorious. It sounded like forever.

"Yes." She wrapped her arms around his neck. "Yes, Garrick. I'll be your wife."

Amanda scanned the grounds of Cedar Ridge as she reached the top of the steep, pitted road. The midmorning sun fell gently on the shimmering vineyard and warmed the old redwood walls of the main building. The only vestiges of the enormous party that had taken place the night before were a few deep-rutted tire tracks and some trampled grass. She flexed her fingers over the steering wheel. Ah, yes, there was one other. The square-cut diamond on the third finger of her left hand caught the sunshine glaring through the windshield and scattered it into a thousand tiny rainbows.

As her pickup truck clattered into the dusty driveway, Garrick strolled out onto the veranda, clutching a mug of coffee. His T-shirt was untucked, his hair amuss; his well-worn jeans hugged his strong thighs. He leaned against the trellis and smiled that wonderful baseball-player grin as she tumbled out of her truck and adjusted her sunglasses against the glare.

"Well, Kane, you did it again."

A newspaper sailed through the air and landed at his feet. He looked down at it. "Uh-oh."

"Read it." She swung her purse over her shoulder and climbed the stairs. "Read it and weep."

Garrick opened the paper; it was folded to page 6. He groaned as he sank to the top stair of the veranda. It was Sadie Cello's column.

CAGEY KANE CORRALS KARLSON

You heard it here first, my curious friends! Last night, at the posh opening of the Cedar Ridge Winery, Ms. Amanda "The Ice Queen" Karlson agreed to tie the knot with none other than her boss, ex-playboy Mr. Garrick Kane. Frankly, this little birdie doubted that even the charming rock-climber could find a foothold in that glacier, but apparently practice makes perfect! Just goes to show you what I've suspected all along—there's been more than one kind of fermentation going on in that little mountain ravine this season . . . and true love conquers all . . .

Garrick looked at her sidelong. "Looks like we got some more free publicity."

Amanda shrugged and suppressed her smile.

"You had to expect this," he argued. "It isn't everyday an owner and a winemaster decide to tie the knot—and announce it at their own opening."

"Hmm."

He caught the glimmer in her eye. The corners of Amanda's lips twitched, then, unable to pretend any longer, she broke into a smile. She had brought the article this morning on purpose. Sadie Cello and her ilk couldn't hurt her anymore; no one could hurt her. She wanted Garrick to know that. With Garrick's love, she felt invincible.

Garrick put his coffee aside to clutch her to him and kiss her hard and fast on the mouth. She kissed him back, but as the kiss deepened, lengthened, she gently pulled away and nodded behind them, to the half-open door. He groaned and curled his fingers into hers.

"Damn the Kane clan for infesting this house." He squeezed her hand. "I missed you this morning."

"Mmm. I missed you, too."

"Come Tuesday, Amanda love, you're moving in until the spring wedding."

"Am I?" She tilted her head, letting the sweep of her unbound hair shimmer over her shoulder. "That'll be just in time for the arrival of my family. My mother, my sister Karen and her kids are flying in on Wednesday, and Rachel is joining us as soon as her assignment is over in Milan."

"Are you telling me I have to pass the rigid standards of three *more* Karlson women?"

"Don't worry about it. My state of spinsterhood has been a source of endless discussion among those Karlson women." Her lips twisted in a wry grin. "When I spoke to them this morning, I got the impression they'd welcome you into the family if your name was Snake and you were covered with tattoos."

"I always did want to buy a motorcycle . . ."

"Over my dead body, Kane."

He kissed her teasingly, the taste of coffee fresh on his lips. "Come on. My family is chomping at the bit. They'll come out and get us if we don't go in soon."

She tugged him down as he tried to rise. "Can't we just sit here for a while? Enjoy the view?"

"Amanda . . ."

"I know." She wrinkled her nose. "I'm stalling."

"You shouldn't." He settled back down beside her. "They'll love you as much as I do."

She laid her head on his shoulder and wondered if she would ever get used to hearing those words. She sighed and gazed over the green, fertile vineyards, and listened to the sound of the birds chattering in the oak trees that shaded the house.

"What is it?" He hugged her close. "You're a hundred miles away."

"More like three thousand." Her expression mellowed, turned dreamy. "Ever since last night I can't seem to stop thinking about a little farmhouse in the foothills of the Berkshires."

Garrick watched her face as her gaze roamed with open admiration over the hills of Cedar Ridge. "Does our winery remind you of home?"

She didn't answer right away. From inside the house came the noise of his family talking and arguing and laughing; the sound of dishes clattering and pots bubbling on the stove, the quick and light feet of children running wild. The scent of sizzling bacon and sausage wafted heavily through the half-open door.

"No, it doesn't remind me of home." She turned and looked deep into his eyes. "Today, and from now on, Garrick . . . it *is* home."

SHARE THE FUN . . .
SHARE YOUR NEW-FOUND TREASURE!!

You don't want to let your new books out of your sight? That's okay. Your friends can get their own. Order below.

No. 93 NO LIMIT TO LOVE by Kate Freiman
Lisa was called the "little boss" and Bruiser didn't like it one bit!

No. 94 SPECIAL EFFECTS by Jo Leigh
Catlin wouldn't fall for any tricks from Luke, the master of illusion.

No. 95 PURE INSTINCT by Ellen Fletcher
She tried but Amie couldn't forget Buck's strong arms and teasing lips.

No. 96 THERE IS A SEASON by Phyllis Houseman
The heat of the volcano rivaled the passion between Joshua and Beth.

No. 97 THE STILLMAN CURSE by Peggy Morse
Leandra thought revenge would be sweet. Todd had sweeter things in mind.

No. 98 BABY MAKES FIVE by Lacey Dancer
Cait could say 'no' to his business offer but not to Robert, the man.

No. 99 MOON SHOWERS by Laura Phillips
Both Sam and the historic Missouri home quickly won Hilary's heart.

No. 100 GARDEN OF FANTASY by Karen Rose Smith
If Beth wasn't careful, she'd fall into the arms of her enemy, Nash.